* 1,000,000 *

Free E-Books

@

www.ForgottenBooks.org

* Alchemy *

The Secret is Revealed

@

www.TheBookofAquarius.com

Forgotten Books

Judas Iscariot

Formings With Eleazar (Lazarus), and Ben a Biblical Trilogy

By

Leonid Andreyev

Published by Forgotten Books 2012
Originally Published 1910

PIBN 1000124936

Copyright © 2012 Forgotten Books
www.forgottenbooks.org

JUDAS ISCARIOT

JUDAS ISCARIOT

Forming, with 'Eleazar' (Lazarus) and 'Ben Tobit,' a Biblical Trilogy

BY

L. N. ANDRÉYEV

TRANSLATED FROM THE RUSSIAN
BY W. H. LOWE
Rector of Brisley, Norfolk
AUTHOR OF 'SYSTEMIZATION OF THE RUSSIAN VERB,' ETC.

London
FRANCIS GRIFFITHS
34, MAIDEN LANE, STRAND, W.C.
1910

Richard Clay & Sons, Limited,
Bread Street Hill, E.C. and
Bungay, Suffolk.

INTRODUCTION

OUR author, Leonid N. Andreyev, is not to be confounded with the musician, "M. Andreeff," who has lately been taking the London Coliseum by storm with his Balalaïka Court Orchestra. But he is already known to a limited public in England as author of *The Red Laugh* and *The Seven who were Hanged*. Besides plays, etc., he has produced a considerable number of short stories. As a rule he chooses everyday subjects, set as is but natural in Russian surroundings, but still of universal human interest. It is only in these three stories, which I have ventured to put together as a " Biblical Trilogy," that he has treated of biblical subjects, and has transported his readers to Palestine and Rome.

Biblical subjects are always of interest to

the English reader. At the same time, there are many who may deem it irreverent to treat of the Gospels in the form of a romance. One can sympathize with such objectors, although feeling bound to disagree with them. For there would seem to be a distinct advantage afforded by this imaginative treatment. Does not the constant reading of the acts and words of JESUS and His disciples in the same familiar language tend to stereotype the narrative, and so cause one to forget that the Gospel characters were men of like passions with ourselves, and not mere lay-figures on which to hang certain doctrines? When, on the other hand, one reads such romances as *Ben Hur*, Renan's *Vie de Jesus*, *Barabbas*, or *Judas Iscariot*, the scenes become more vivid and real, and the characters stand out in their individual distinctness, so that, even though one may not, perhaps, agree with the views of the particular writer, the perusal of the romances is never without its peculiar profit

But these tales must be approached in a

INTRODUCTION vii

somewhat different spirit to that in which one would view most of those mentioned above. For the treatment here is more than usually unconventional. The reader must prepare himself for shocks—shocks to his æsthetic taste—shocks to his religious susceptibilities.

To take, as is only right, the religious side first. In these stories JESUS is represented merely as the *Man* Christ Jesus.

The opening words of " Judas " proclaim : Ecce Homo; for we are told that JESUS had been long " warned " against Judas, whereas in John vi. 70 we read, that He foreknew that one of His Apostles was a devil.

And so throughout the story He is looked on as a mere human teacher; but nothing is ever said about His life and teaching which is not consistent with the profoundest respect and appreciation.

In " Eleazar " the Power of Christ as the efficient cause of the resurrection of Lazarus is simply ignored. And that, evidently, with intention; for he is always referred to as one who had miraculously risen (*voskresshy*), not as one miraculously raised (*voskreshonny*) from the dead. And herein seems to lie the secret of the disastrous results of his resurrection. The believer, meditating on the subject, pictures to himself a form restored to at least all its original comeliness; he imagines the joy of the sisters, and of the friends and neighbours of Lazarus at his restoration. And though he may wish that Lazarus had brought back some message from the land of shadows, he consoles himself with the thought that it was perhaps necessary that he should return in complete oblivion of what he had gone through, or that—maybe for some inscrutable purpose—he had been forbidden to reveal his experiences. Be this as it may, the believer can imagine none but good results to [1] all concerned as accruing from the resurrection of Lazarus from the dead.

Therefore the horrible idea conceived by L. Andreyev is indeed a shock to him.

But is it not in reality rather a consolation,

or at all events a warning? For is not this distorted view of the case simply the result of unbelief? Had our author been a believer in the Power of the Resurrection, he would certainly have written otherwise than he has written.

Even in "Ben Tobit" one may find this same rationalism; for, in addition to the *motif* suggested by its opening sentence, there seems to underlie the story an assumption that the Crucifixion of JESUS was, to the ordinary inhabitant of Jerusalem, no more than the punishment of a common felon. "See," says Sarah, "the criminals are going by to execution."

Thus the standpoint of the writer in all three stories is the reverse of orthodox.

But offences against taste are even more numerous than those against orthodoxy. Indeed, taste (at all events from the Englishman's point of view) is, I fear, conspicuous by its absence from most of the works of L. Andreyev; but there is no need to emphasize here this defect, by quoting passages which one felt some reluctance even in translating.

L. Andreyev is a decadent, and we cannot expect him to be free from the defects of that school.

"Eleazar" is a gruesome tale, though none, I think, will deny that it is powerful; but still it is too strained to be convincing, and leaves such an uncomfortable impression on the mind that one cannot forbear asking, "After all: cui bono?" If it be intended for believers of the Gospel—can it please them? If it be meant for the benefit of unbelievers, it reveals nothing, and will only sink them deeper in the slough of despond. Can it be that it is written merely as a *Tour de force*, to produce "a fresh thrill," to maintain or to enhance the author's reputation for the weird? Whatever be its intention, it can hardly (in spite of the extravagant views entertained of its greatness by many in Russia) be regarded as one of his happiest inspirations.

As a matter of fact, in this tale he has

INTRODUCTION xi

undertaken a task beyond the powers of man. For what mere human intellect is competent to fathom the mysteries of Life and Death? Indeed it was—one cannot but think—an instinctive consciousness of the limitations of genius, which had, hitherto, withheld novelists from attempting to relate the history of Lazarus after his resurrection.

There are, however, glimpses of Hope in this "Dance of Death." The exquisitely chiselled butterfly—its wings fluttering in an impotent attempt to fly—found under the most "wildly shrieking" projection of the ugly piece of statuary, is a well-known emblem of the resurrection; and may here amid the fragments of the shattered statue signify that which he so poetically expresses in his "Splendid is the life for them that are rerisen," viz. that "men may rise on stepping-stones of their dead selves to higher things."

Or the butterfly may be taken as a symbol of the Ideal, which all strive after, but to which few, if any, attain. This thought he has expressed under the figure of " The Little Angel " in his story of that name. But whatever its special significance may be, it is evident that it was the butterfly which enabled the sculptor to reply to his friends' inquiries: " Eureka ! "

In the hardly-won victory of the mighty Cæsar over the enervating power of Lazarus redivivus, we seem to recognize here, as elsewhere, the influence of Friedrich Nietzsche. Here is depicted a concrete example of the power of Dionysus, the " Will to live." Struggle and Victory, as lauded in the rhapsody of Tiberius, are the very key-note of the philosophy of F. Nietzsche; viz. the struggle of the Individual—at all costs—to produce by evolution the Super-man. This " at all costs " provides the explanation of the brutality of Tiberius in putting out the eyes of Lazarus. The eyes of Lazarus were baleful—therefore they must perish. For Friedrich Nietzsche preferred (or pretended to

INTRODUCTION   xiii

prefer) the cruel opportunism of a Tiberius to the tender humanity of Christ. Indeed, he ventured to write that, if JESUS had lived longer, He would have outlived His own teaching, and that He was great enough to have retracted it!

A mere external resemblance to Nietzsche is also observable in Lazarus, and some of his victims—viz. that of gazing at the light of the sun, as though to them, as to the ancient Greeks, οραν φαος ηελίοιο was a synonym for being alive. But possibly this last supposition may be too strained. For to all "truly the light is sweet, and a pleasant thing it is for the eyes to behold the sun," and I must plead guilty to being myself somewhat of a Parsee, and that possibly on account of the rarity with which we of Northern climes "see the light of the sun," as D. Von Visin (I think it is) laments, that one so fond of sunlight and beautiful scenery as himself should have been doomed to be born on the banks of the frozen Neva.

The full title of Judas Iscariot is "Judas Iscariot, and others." Among the "others" are Jesus, Peter, James, John, Matthew, Thomas, Mary of Bethany, Mary of Magdala, Annas, Caiaphas, Pontius Pilate, the Sanhedrin, soldiers, servants, etc. Of the secondary characters, Peter and Thomas are the most interesting. The bluff honesty of the Galilean fisherman is strongly depicted, while the owl-like stupidity of Thomas is well sustained throughout. Matthew is ponderous, and for some reason, known perhaps to the author, he is represented as continually quoting "Solomon"; John, the Beloved Disciple, is disappointing, being represented as caustic and supercilious, not altogether too lovable, and indeed something of a prig; and Mary Magdalene seems to be introduced chiefly as a foil to Judas. In this connection there are some passages which I would willingly have modified, or deleted, but could not do so without injustice to the author.

The physical ugliness of Judas is an in-

INTRODUCTION

stance of L. Andreyev's love of the grotesque. There was no moral necessity for representing him as a monstrosity, since devils too often appear as angels of light. Leonardo da Vinci did not deem it necessary to make him a monster of ugliness, but was satisfied to paint him in his "Last Supper" as a typical Jew. It is possible, however, that our author had in mind "the ugliest man" of F. Nietzsche, whose deed was as ugly as that imputed by prophecy to Judas in the latter-day legends.

Although avarice is no longer regarded as the motive of the Betrayal, lying, thieving, and hypocrisy are still insisted on as part of the very complex character of Judas. In the scene in which he bargains with Annas, it would appear that greed took no part in his scheme. He seems, rather, with his peculiar, malicious irony, to be simply baiting the astute Annas. But when, on returning the thirty pieces of silver to the Sanhedrin, he discovers that he had not deceived them after all and that they knew, as well as he did, that

INTRODUCTION

Jesus was the most innocent of men, then his cloak of lifelong hypocrisy falls from him, and, at last, he appears as he is.

In the fiery words of contempt hurled by Judas on the eleven for their cowardice in deserting their Master, we see the Russian patriot a-blaze. Christianity has condoned the desertion in consideration of the courage shown in after years; and softly-nurtured Westerns, steeped in selfishness, whose forebears bore for them the burden and heat of the day, may look on the act as excusable. But can it be a matter of surprise that one of a nation always ready to suffer torture and death for a Cause, one too of the class from which the majority of its victims are drawn, should put words of such withering scorn into the mouth of the Traitor—who at all events had the courage of his opinions?

But all of this is mere detail. The absorbing theme of interest throughout the Drama is the love of Judas for Jesus, and his jealous desire to be first in His affections,

Then why mention it?

which culminates in madness, and the consequent betrayal of his beloved Master to death, and his own "free death" (as Nietzsche calls suicide), in order that "whither He is gone, he may follow Him"—not "hereafter"—but at once.

This brings us to the motives of Judas for betraying his Master, which have much exercised the thoughts of theologians.

Indeed, at first sight, it may seem strange that the services of a traitor should be required at all, since JESUS had taught "daily in the temple, and they had laid no hands on Him." The object, however, of such a device seems to have been, to enable the soldiers to seize Him suddenly and quietly in the night, "lest there should be an uproar among the people."

The motive most commonly imputed to Judas is avarice; inasmuch as in John xii. 12 he is mentioned as a "thief, who held the bag." But surely a paltry sum of thirty pieces of silver (between two and three pounds of our present-day money) would hardly have

INTRODUCTION

tempted the meanest specimen of a thief (says L. Andreyev's *vor*) to betray such a Master, after associating with Him so long and so intimately! *[handwritten: This is difficult for a peaceable [?] brained anti-semite translator to understand.]*

The second supposition—that Judas wished to force his Master into avowing Himself to be the Messiah—seems much more probable. L. Andreyev's is a modification of this latter view. He would make it appear that jealousy of Peter and John was the final cause of the betrayal. Judas loved JESUS intensely; more courageously than Peter, more passionately than John. Hence he could not bear to take an inferior place in his Master's affections. Towards the end of our Lord's life upon earth, even the apostles seem to have desponded of the immediate establishment of the Kingdom of Heaven. Hence the Kingdom of Heaven began already to be looked upon as belonging to a Future State. The struggle between the apostles was to be "first" in the Kingdom of Heaven. Judas is represented here as having thought that the

INTRODUCTION

first to enter the unseen world after JESUS, would secure the first place in dignity. And so—utterly insane as he had now become—he causes JESUS to be put to death, and then, by hanging himself, assures his own arrival in the Kingdom of Heaven, immediately after Him. The mad self-complacency of Judas after the Crucifixion is very finely depicted.

The gradual growth of madness is here, as in a large number of our author's tales, the theme of his study, and will, no doubt, at the hands of the reviewers, meet with a much fuller analysis than has been possible in these few pages.

Such is Andreyev's attempt to "white-wash," as some of his critics have said, the character of the Traitor; and it must be admitted, that his solution of the difficulty is as good as any that has yet been offered. In propounding it, L. Andreyev shows once more his intense human sympathy, and proclaims that even the Traitor Judas was also "a man."

"Ben Tobit" is a simple little tale containing a graphic description of toothache; as any reader who has ever suffered from that "wimbling" torment will readily testify. The *motif* of the story is contained in the opening sentence: "On the day when the world's great crime was consummated, Ben Tobit was suffering from toothache," that is to say, that even when the most stupendous events are taking place, the trivial incidents of daily life still engross the thoughts of individuals. A trite enough thought, but here redeemed from the commonplace by the gracefully simple manner in which the story is told.

L. Andreyev is intensely realistic, and what is more, his realism and power of description amount to absolute genius. Sometimes, by a masterly touch of the pen, he gives us an impressionist picture, as when, in "Eleazar," he so vividly describes in a few lines the busy streets of Rome. At others, he paints his scene with a wonderful minuteness of detail, never wearisome, ever truthfully conceived. Moreover, he is a sincere lover of nature, and is often able, at will, with one dash of the pen to conjure before the mind an elysium, or a very hell, of sight, or smell, or sound, or feeling; or to suggest a whole world of mystery (as in his frequent allusions to spring-time). Thus it comes about that, forgetful of his decadence, one can always read his pages with "that emotional delight, and elevated pleasure," which is the criterion of true art.

Good taste is more or less an innate quality, while literary style depends chiefly upon education. Nevertheless, style is not an easy thing to criticize on account of the difficulty of establishing a satisfactory criterion. If one takes personal feeling, one is pretty sure to go wrong, while if one accepts contemporary opinion as one's standard, one runs the risk of falling out of the Scylla of private judgment into the Charybdis of popular error. Therefore, I content myself with saying that

L. Andreyev has a style entirely his own, and it must be accepted as such. Still one cannot but anticipate that contemporary opinion will take exception to his habit of reiterating expressions descriptive of his characters, such as "like a one-eyed demon," "as though he had not two, but a whole dozen (*lit.* a decade of) feet," "him who had miraculously risen from the dead," "had been three days in the enigmatical power of death," "me the leper," etc.

Now Count L. Tolstoy, in comparing himself with Pushkin as an artist, said, that amongst others one of the differences between them was this, that Pushkin in depicting a characteristic detail does it lightly, not troubling himself whether it be noticed or understood by the reader, while he himself stood over the reader, as it were, with this artistic detail, until he had set it forth distinctly. Upon this D. Merejkowski[1] remarks (*inter alia*): "It seems as if Pushkin . . . gave

[1] *Tolstoy and Dostoievki as artists*, chap. ix.

little that we might want the more. . . . But Tolstoy gives so much that there is nothing more for us to want; we are sated if not glutted." To which I would take leave to add: that L. Andreyev gives us no more than we want (though perhaps more than would be allowed to an English writer), and so, in a word, as a Russian he hits off the exact golden mean between the styles of Pushkin and Tolstoy.

The serious reader is entreated, before undertaking the perusal of these stories, to endeavour to divest his mind of all theological prejudice and personal bias, so as to bring it into a state of perfect receptivity, as the photographer's plate must be free of all dust and flaws, if it is to receive a faithful image of the object before it. So only will he be able to enjoy the drama of Judas, to tolerate the tragedy of Eleazar, and to smile indulgently at the homely picture of Ben Tobit, the merchant of Jerusalem.

I am indebted to my friend Mr. Z. N.

Preev, London correspondent to the *Novaya Russ*, the S. Petersburg *Revue des Theatres*, and the Odessa *Novosty*, for kindly running through my translations with me.

W. H. L.

January 1910.

JUDAS ISCARIOT

I

Jesus Christ had often been warned that Judas Iscariot was a man of very evil repute, and that He ought to beware of him. Some of the disciples, who had been in Judæa, knew him well, while others had heard much about him from various sources, and there was none who had a good word for him. If good people in speaking of him blamed him, as covetous, cunning, and inclined to hypocrisy and lying, the bad, when asked concerning him, inveighed against him in the severest terms.

"He is always making mischief between us," they would say, and spit in contempt. "He has always some thought which he keeps to himself. He creeps into a house quietly, like a scorpion, but goes out again with an ostentatious noise. There are friends among thieves, and comrades among robbers, and even liars have wives, to whom they speak the truth; but Judas laughs at thieves and honest folk alike, although he is himself a clever thief. Moreover, he is in appearance the ugliest person in Judæa. No! he is no friend of ours, this foxy-haired Judas Iscariot," the bad would say, thereby surprising the good people, in whose opinion there was not much difference between him and all other vicious people in Judæa. They would recount further how that he had long ago deserted his wife, who was living in poverty and misery, striving to eke out a living from the unfruitful patch of land which constituted his estate. That he had wandered for many years aimlessly among the people, and had even gone from one sea to the other,—no mean distance, —and that everywhere he lied and grimaced, and would make some discovery with his thievish eye, and then would suddenly disappear, leaving behind him animosity and strife. Yes, he was as inquisitive, artful and hateful as a one-eyed demon. Children he had none, and this was an additional proof that Judas was a wicked man, that God would not have from him any posterity.

None of the disciples had noticed when it was that this ugly, foxy-haired Jew [1] first appeared in the company of Christ: but he had for a long time haunted their path, joined in their conversations, performed little acts of service, bowing and smiling and currying favour. Sometimes they became quite used to him, so that he escaped their weary eyes; at others he would suddenly obtrude himself on eye and ear, irritating them as something abnormally ugly, treacherous and disgusting. Then they would drive him away with severe words, and for a short time he would disappear, only to reappear suddenly, officious, flattering and crafty as a one-eyed demon.

[1] Judas was the only one of the original Twelve who came from Judæa. The others were Galilæans.—*Tr.*

There was no doubt in the minds of some of the disciples that under his desire to draw near to Jesus was hidden some secret intention —some malign and cunning scheme.

But Jesus did not listen to their advice, their prophetic voice did not reach His ears. In that spirit of serene contradiction, which ever irresistibly inclined Him to the reprobate and unlovable, He deliberately accepted Judas, and included him in the circle of the chosen. The disciples were disturbed and murmured under their breath, but He would sit still, with His face towards the setting sun, and listen abstractedly, perhaps to them, perhaps to something else. For ten days there had been no wind, and the transparent atmosphere, listening and sensitive, continued ever the same, motionless and unchanged. It seemed as though it preserved in its transparent depths every cry and song made during those days by men and beasts and birds— tears, laments and cheerful song, prayer and cursings—and that on account of these crystallized sounds it was, that the air was so heavy, threatening, and saturated with invisible life. Once more the sun was sinking. It rolled heavily downwards in a flaming ball, setting on fire the sky. Everything upon the earth which was turned towards it: the swarthy face of Jesus, the walls of the houses, and the leaves of the trees—everything obediently reflected that distant fearfully pensive light. Now the white walls were no longer white, and the white city upon the white hill was turned to red.

And lo! Judas arrived. He arrived bowing low, bending his back, cautiously and timidly protruding his ugly, bumpy head — just exactly such as his acquaintances had described. He was spare and of good height, almost the same as that of Jesus, who stooped a little through the habit of thinking as He walked, and so appeared shorter than He was. Judas was to all appearance fairly strong and well knit, though for some reason or other he pretended to be weak and somewhat sickly. He had an uncertain voice. Sometimes it was strong and manly, at others shrill as that of an old woman scolding her husband, provokingly thin, and disagreeable to the ear, so that ofttimes one felt inclined to tear out his words from the ear, like rough, decaying splinters. His short red locks failed to hide the curious unusual form of his skull. It looked as if it had been split at the nape of the neck by a double sword-cut, and then joined together again, so that it was apparently divided into four parts, and inspired distrust, nay, even alarm: for behind such a cranium there could be no quiet or concord, but there must ever be heard the noise of sanguinary and merciless strife. The face of Judas was similarly doubled. One side of it, with a black, sharply watchful eye, was vivid and mobile, readily gathering into innumerable tortuous wrinkles. On the other side were no wrinkles, it was deadly flat, smooth, and set, and though of the same size as the other it seemed enormous on account of its wide-open blind eye.

Covered with a whitish film, closing neither night nor day, this eye met light and darkness with the same indifference, but perhaps on account of the proximity of its lively and crafty companion it never got full credit for blindness.

When in a paroxysm of joy or excitement Judas closed his sound eye and shook his head, the other eye would always shake in unison and gaze in silence. Even people quite devoid of penetration could clearly perceive, when looking at Judas, that such a man could bring no good. . . .

And yet Jesus brought him near to Himself, and once even made him sit next to Him. John, the beloved disciple, fastidiously moved away, and all the others who loved their Teacher cast down their eyes in disapprobation. But Judas sat on, and turning his head from side to side, began in a somewhat thin voice to complain of ill-health, and how that his chest gave him pain in the night, and that when ascending a hill he got out of breath, and when he stood still on the edge of a precipice he would be seized with a dizziness, and could scarcely restrain a foolish desire to throw himself down. And many other impious things he invented, as though not understanding that sicknesses do not come to a man by chance, but as a consequence of conduct not corresponding with the laws of the Eternal. This Judas Iscariot kept on rubbing his chest with his broad palm, and even pretended to cough, midst a general silence and downcast eyes.

John, without looking at the Teacher, whispered to his friend Simon Peter—

"Aren't you tired of that lie? I can't stand it any longer, I am going away."

Peter glanced at Jesus, and meeting his eye, quickly stood up.

"Wait a moment," said he to his friend.

Once more he looked at Jesus; sharply as a stone torn from a mountain moved towards Judas, and said to him in a loud voice, with expansive, serene courtesy—

"You will come with us, Judas."

He gave him a kindly slap on his bent back, and without looking at the Teacher, though he felt His eye upon him, resolutely added in his loud voice, which excluded all objection, just as water excludes air—

"It does not matter that you have such a nasty face. There fall into our nets even worse monstrosities, and they sometimes turn out very tasty to eat. It is not for us, our Lord's fishermen, to throw away a catch, merely because the fish have spines, or only one eye. I saw once at Tyre an octopus, which had been caught by the local fishermen, and I was so frightened that I wanted to run away. But they laughed at me, a fisherman from Tiberias; and gave me some of it to eat, and I asked for more, it was so tasty. You remember, Master, that I told you the story, and you laughed, too. And you, Judas, are like an octopus—but only on one side."

And he laughed loudly, content with his joke. When Peter spoke, his words resounded so forcibly, that it was as though he were driving them in with nails. When Peter moved, or did anything, he made a noise that could be heard afar, and which called forth a response from the deafest of things: the stone floor rumbled under his feet, the doors shook and rattled, and the very air was convulsed with fear, and roared. In the clefts of the mountains his voice awoke the inmost echo, and in the morning-time, when they were fishing on the lake, he would roll himself about on the sleepy, glittering water, and force the first shy sunbeams into smiles.

For this apparently he was loved: when on all other faces there still lay the shadow of night, his powerful head, and bare breast, and freely extended arms were already aglow with the light of dawn.

The words of Peter, evidently approved as they were by the Master, dispersed the oppressive atmosphere. But some of the disciples, who had been to the seaside and had seen an octopus, were disturbed by its monstrous image being so lightly applied to the new disciple. They recalled the immense eyes, the dozens of greedy tentacles, the feigned repose—and then all at once! it embraced, clung round, crushed and sucked out, and that without one wink of its monstrous eyes. What was it? But Jesus remained silent. He smiled with a frown of kindly raillery on Peter, who was still telling glowing tales about the octopus. Then one by one the disciples shame-facedly approached Judas, and began a friendly conversation with him, but—beat a hasty and awkward retreat.

Only John the son of Zebedee maintained an obstinate silence; and Thomas had evidently not made up his mind to say anything, but was still weighing the matter. He kept his gaze attentively fixed on Christ and Judas as they sat together. And that strange proximity of divine beauty and monstrous ugliness, of a man with a benign look, and of an octopus with immense, motionless, dully greedy eyes, oppressed his mind like an insoluble enigma.

He tensely wrinkled his smooth, upright

forehead, and screwed up his eyes, thinking that so he would see better, but only succeeded in imagining that Judas really had eight incessantly moving feet. But that was not true. Thomas understood that, and again obstinately gazed.

Judas gathered courage: he straightened out his arms, which had been bent at the elbows, relaxed the muscles which held his jaws in tension, and began cautiously to protrude his bumpy head into the light. It had been all along in view of all, but Judas imagined that it had been impenetrably hidden from sight by some invisible, but thick and cunning veil. But lo! now, as though creeping out from a ditch, he felt his strange skull, and then his eyes, in the light: he stopped and then deliberately exposed his whole face. Nothing happened; Peter had gone away somewhere or other. Jesus sat pensive, with His head leaning on His hand, and gently swayed His sunburnt foot. The disciples were conversing together, and only Thomas gazed at him attentively and seriously, like a conscientious tailor taking measurement. Judas smiled; Thomas did not reply to the smile; but evidently took it into account, as he did everything else, and continued to gaze. But something unpleasant alarmed the left side of Judas' countenance as he looked round. John, handsome, pure, without a single fleck upon his snow-white conscience, was looking at him out of a dark corner, with cold but beautiful eyes. And though he walked as others walk, yet Judas felt as if he were dragging himself along the ground like a whipped cur, as he went up to John and said: " Why are you silent, John? Your words are like golden apples in vessels of silver filigree work: bestow one of them on Judas, who is so poor."

John looked steadfastly into his wide-open motionless eye, and said nothing. And he looked on, while Judas crept out, hesitated a moment, and then disappeared in the deep darkness of the open door.

Since the full moon was up, there were many people out walking. Jesus went out too, and from the low roof on which Judas had spread his couch he saw them going out. In the light of the moon each white figure looked light, and deliberate in its movements; and seemed not so much to walk as to glide in front of its dark shadow. Then suddenly a man would be lost in something black, and his voice became audible. And when people once more appeared in the moonlight, they seemed silent—like white walls, or black shadows—as everything did in the transparent mist of night. Almost every one was asleep when Judas heard the soft voice of Jesus returning. All in and round about the house was still. A cock crew; somewhere or other an ass, disturbed in his sleep, brayed aloud and insolently as in daytime, and reluctantly and gradually relapsed into silence. Judas did not sleep at all, but listened surreptitiously. The moon illumined one half of his face, and was reflected strangely in his enormous open eye, as on the frozen surface of a lake.

Suddenly he remembered something, and hastily coughed, rubbing his perfectly healthy chest with his hairy hand: maybe some one was not yet asleep, and was listening to what Judas was thinking!

II

THEY gradually became used to Judas, and ceased to notice his ugliness. Jesus entrusted the common purse to him, and with it there fell on him all household cares: he purchased the necessary food and clothing, distributed alms, and when they were on the road, it was his duty to choose the place where they were to stop, or to find a night's lodging.

All this he did very cleverly, so that in a short time he had earned the goodwill of some of the disciples, who had noticed his efforts. Judas was an habitual liar, but they became used to this, when they found that his lies were not followed by any evil conduct; nay, they added a special piquancy to his conversation and tales, and made life seem like a comic, and sometimes a tragic, tale.

According to his stories he seemed to know every one, and each person that he knew had some time in his life been guilty of evil conduct, or even crime. Those, according to him, were called good, who knew how to conceal their thoughts and acts; but if one only embraced, flattered, and questioned such a man sufficiently, there would ooze out from him every untruth, nastiness, and lie, like matter from a pricked wound. He freely confessed that he sometimes lied himself; but affirmed with an oath that others were still greater liars, and that if any one in this world was ever deceived, it was Judas.

Indeed, according to his own account, he had been deceived, time upon time, in one way or another. Thus, a certain guardian of the treasures of a rich grandee once confessed to him, that he had for ten years been continually on the point of stealing the property committed to him, but that he was debarred by fear of the grandee, and of his own conscience. And Judas believed him—and he suddenly committed the theft, and deceived Judas. But even then Judas still trusted him

—and then he suddenly restored the stolen treasure to the grandee, and again deceived Judas. Yes, everything deceived him, even animals. Whenever he pets a dog it bites his fingers; but when he beats it with a stick it licks his feet, and looks into his eyes like a daughter. He killed one such dog, and buried it deep, laying a great stone on the top of it—but who knows? Perhaps just because he killed it, it has come to life again, and instead of lying in the trench, is running about cheerfully with other dogs.

All laughed merrily at Judas' tale, and he smiled pleasantly himself, winking his one lively mocking eye—and by that very smile confessed that he had lied somewhat; that he had not really killed the dog. But he would infallibly find it and kill it, because he did not wish to be deceived. And at these words of Judas they laughed all the more.

But sometimes in his tales he transgressed the bounds of probability, and ascribed to people such proclivities as even the beasts do not possess, accusing them of such crimes as are not, and never have been. And since he named in this connection the most honoured people, some were indignant at the calumny, while others jokingly asked—

"How about your own father and mother, Judas—were they not good people?"

Judas winked his eye, and smiled with a gesture of his hands. And the fixed, wide-open eye shook in unison with the shaking of his head, and looked out in silence.

"But who was my father? Perhaps it was the man who used to beat me with a rod, or may be—a devil, a goat or a cock. . . . How can Judas tell? How can Judas tell with whom his mother shared her couch. Judas had many fathers; which of them do you refer to?"

But at this they were all indignant, for they had a profound reverence for parents; and Matthew, who was very learned in the scriptures, said severely in the words of Solomon—

"Whoso slandereth his father and his

mother, his lamp shall be extinguished in deep darkness."

But John the son of Zebedee haughtily jerked out: "And what of us? What evil have you to say of us, Judas Iscariot?"

But he waved his hands in simulated terror, whined, and bowed like a beggar, who has in vain asked an alms of a passer-by: "Ah! they are tempting poor Judas! They are laughing at him, they wish to take in the poor, trusting Judas!" And while one side of his face was crinkled up in buffooning grimaces, the other side wagged seriously and severely, and the never-closing eye looked out in a broad stare.

More and louder than any laughed Simon Peter at the jokes of Judas Iscariot. But once it happened that he suddenly frowned, and became silent and sad, and hastily dragging Judas aside by the sleeve, he bent down, and asked in a hoarse whisper—

"But Jesus? What do you think of Jesus? Speak seriously, I entreat you."

Judas cast on him a malign glance.

"And what do you think?"

Peter whispered with awe and gladness—

"I think that He is the son of the living God."

"Then why do you ask? What can Judas tell you, whose father was a goat!"

"But do you love Him? You do not seem to love any one, Judas."

And with the same strange malignity Iscariot blurted out abruptly and sharply: "I do."

Some two days after this conversation Peter openly dubbed Judas "his friend the octopus"; but Judas awkwardly, and ever with the same malignity, endeavoured to creep away from him into some dark corner, and would sit there morosely glaring with his white, never-closing eye.

Thomas alone took him quite seriously. He understood nothing of jokes, hypocrisy or lies, nor of the play upon words and thoughts, but investigated everything positively to the very bottom. He would often interrupt Judas' stories about wicked people and their conduct with short practical remarks—

"You must prove that. Did you hear it yourself? Was there any one present besides yourself? What was his name?"

At this Judas would get angry, and shrilly cry out, that he had seen and heard everything himself; but the obstinate Thomas would go on cross-examining quietly and pertinaciously, until Judas confessed that he had lied, or until he invented some new and more probable lie, which provided the others for some time with food for thought. But when Thomas found out a discrepancy, he immediately would come and calmly expose the liar.

Usually Judas excited in him a strong curiosity, which brought about between them a sort of friendship, full of wrangling, jeering, and invective on the one side, and of quiet insistence on the other. Sometimes Judas felt an unbearable aversion to his strange friend, and, transfixing him with a sharp glance, would say irritably, and almost with entreaty—

"What do you want more? I have told you all."

"I want you to prove how it is possible that a he-goat should be your father," Thomas would reply with calm insistency, and wait for an answer.

It chanced once, that after such a question, Judas suddenly left off speaking and gazed at him with surprise from head to foot. What he saw was a tall, upright figure, a grey face, honest eyes of transparent blue, two fat folds beginning at the nose and losing themselves in a stiff, evenly-trimmed beard. He said with conviction—

"What a stupid you are, Thomas! What do you dream about—a tree, a wall, or a donkey?"

Thomas was in some way strangely purturbed, and made no reply. But at night, when Judas was already closing his vivid, restless eye for sleep, he suddenly said aloud from where he lay—the two now slept together on the roof—

"You are wrong, Judas. I have very bad dreams. What think you? Are people responsible for their dreams?"

"Does, then, any one but the dreamer see a dream?" Judas replied.

Thomas sighed gently, and became thoughtful. But Judas smiled contemptuously, and closed firmly his roguish eye, and quickly gave himself up to his mutinous dreams, monstrous ravings, mad phantoms, which rent his bumpy skull to pieces.

When, during Jesus' travels about Judæa, the travellers approached a village, Iscariot would speak evil of the inhabitants and foretell misfortune. But almost always it happened that the people, of whom he had spoken evil, met Christ and His friends with gladness, and surrounded them with attentions and love, and became believers, and Judas' money-box became so full that it was difficult to carry. And when they laughed at his mistake, he would make a humble gesture with his hands, and say—

"Well, well; Judas thought that they were bad, and they turned out to be good. They quickly believed, and gave money. That only means that Judas has been deceived once more, the poor, confiding Judas Iscariot!"

But on one occasion, when they had already gone far from a village, which had welcomed them kindly, Thomas and Judas began a hot dispute, to settle which they turned back, and did not overtake Jesus and His disciples until the next day. Thomas wore a perturbed and sorrowful appearance, while Judas had such a proud look, that you would have thought that he expected them to offer him their congratulations and thanks upon the spot. Approaching the Master, Thomas declared with decision : " Judas was right, Lord. They were ill-disposed, stupid people. And the seed of your words has fallen upon the rock." And he related what had happened in the village.

JUDAS ISCARIOT

After Jesus and His disciples left it an old woman had begun to cry out that her little white kid had been stolen, and she laid the theft at the door of the visitors who had just departed. At first the people had disputed with her, but when she obstinately insisted that there was no one else who could have done it except Jesus, many agreed with her, and even were about to start in pursuit. And although they soon found the kid straying in the underwood, they still decided that Jesus was a deceiver, and possibly a thief.

"So that's what they think of us, is it?" cried Peter, with a snort. "Lord, wilt Thou that I return to those fools, and   "

But Jesus, saying not a word, gazed severely at him, and Peter in silence retired behind the others. And no one ever referred again to the incident, as though it had never occurred, and as though Judas had been proved wrong. In vain did he show himself on all sides, endeavouring to give to his double, crafty, hook-nosed face an expression of modesty. They would not look at him, and if by chance any one did glance at him, it was in a very unfriendly, not to say contemptuous manner.

From that day forward Jesus' treatment of him underwent a strange change. Formerly, for some reason or other, Judas never used to speak directly with Jesus, who never addressed Himself directly to him, but nevertheless would often glance at him with kindly eyes, smile at his rallies, and if He had not seen him for some time, would inquire: "Where is Judas?"

But now He looked at him as if He did not see him, although as before, and indeed more determinedly than formerly, He sought him out with His eyes every time that He began to speak to the disciples or to the people; but He was either sitting with His back to him, so that He was obliged, as it were, to cast His words over His head so as to reach Judas, or else He made as though He did not notice him at all. And whatever He said, though it was one day one thing, and the next day quite another, although it might be the very thing that Judas was thinking, it always seemed as though He were speaking against him. To all He was the tender, beautiful flower, the sweet-smelling rose of Lebanon, but for Judas He left only sharp thorns, as though Judas had neither heart, nor sight, nor smell, and did not understand, even better than any, the beauty of tender, immaculate petals.

"Thomas! Do you like the yellow rose of Lebanon, which has a swarthy countenance and eyes like the roe?" he inquired once of his friend, who replied indifferently—

"Rose? Yes, I like the smell. But I have never heard of a rose with a swarthy countenance and eyes like a roe!"

"What? Do you not know that the polydactylous cactus, which tore your new garment yesterday, has only one beautiful flower, and only one eye?"

But Thomas did not know this, although

only yesterday a cactus had actually caught in his garment and torn it into wretched rags. But then Thomas never did know anything, though he asked questions about everything, and looked so straight with his bright, transparent eyes, through which, as through a pane of Phœnician glass, was visible a wall behind, with a dismal ass tied to it.

Some time later yet another occurrence took place, in which Judas again proved to be in the right.

At a certain village in Judæa, of which Judas had so bad an opinion, that he had advised them to avoid it, they received Christ with hostility, and after His sermon and exposition of hypocrites they burst into fury, and went about to stone Jesus and His disciples. Enemies He had many, and most likely they would have carried out their sinister intention, but for Judas Iscariot. Seized with a mad fear for Jesus, as though seeing already the drops of ruby blood upon His white garment, Judas threw himself in blind fury upon the crowd, scolding, screeching, beseeching, and lying, and thus gave time and opportunity to Jesus and His disciples to escape.

Strikingly active, as though running upon a dozen feet, laughable and terrible in his fury and entreaties, he threw himself madly in front of the crowd and charmed it with a certain strange power. He shouted that the Nazarene was not possessed of a devil, that He was simply an impostor, a thief who loved money as did all His disciples, and even Judas himself : and he rattled the money-box, grimaced, and beseeched, throwing himself on the ground. And by degrees the anger of the crowd changed into laughter and disgust, and they let fall the stones which they had picked up to throw at them.

" They are not fit to die by the hands of an honest person," said they, while others thoughtfully followed the quickly disappearing Judas with their eyes.

Again Judas expected to receive congratulations, praise, and thanks, and made a show of his torn garments, and pretended that he had been beaten; but this time, too, he was egregiously mistaken. The angry Jesus strode on in silence, and even Peter and John did not venture to approach Him: and all, whose eyes fell on Judas in his torn garments and with a face excited with happiness, but still somewhat frightened, repelled him with curt, angry exclamations.

It was just as though he had not saved them all, just as though he had not saved their Teacher, whom they all loved so much.

"Do you want to see some fools?" said he to Thomas, who was thoughtfully walking in the rear. "Look! There they go along the road in a bunch, like a flock of sheep, kicking up the dust. But you are wise, Thomas, you creep on behind, and I, the noble, magnificent Judas, creep on behind like a dirty slave, who has no place by the side of his masters."

"Why do you call yourself magnificent?" asked Thomas in surprise.

"Because I am so," Judas replied with conviction, and he went on talking, giving more details of how he had deceived the enemies of Jesus, and laughed at them and their stupid stones.

"But you told lies," said Thomas.

"Of course I did," quickly assented Iscariot. "I gave them what they asked for, and they gave me in return what I wanted. And what is a lie, my clever Thomas? Would not the death of Jesus be the greatest lie of all?"

"You did not act rightly. Now I believe that a devil is your father. It was he that taught you, Judas."

The face of Judas grew pale, and something suddenly came over Thomas, and as it were a white cloud passed over, and concealed the road and Jesus. With a gentle movement Judas just as suddenly pressed him to himself, pressed closely with a paralysing movement, and whispered in his ear—

"You mean, then, that a devil has instructed me, don't you, Thomas? Well, I saved Jesus. Therefore a devil loves Jesus and has need of Him, and of the truth. Is it not so, Thomas? But then my father was not a devil, but a he-goat. Can a he-goat want Jesus? Eh? And don't you want Him yourselves, and the truth also?"

Angry and slightly frightened, Thomas freed himself with difficulty from the clinging embrace of Judas, and began to stride quickly forward. But he soon slackened his pace as he endeavoured to understand what had taken place.

But Judas crept on gently behind, and gradually came to a standstill. And lo! in the distance the pedestrians became blended into a parti-coloured bunch, so that it was impossible any longer to distinguish which among those little figures was Jesus. And lo! the little Thomas, too, changed into a grey spot, and suddenly—all disappeared round a turn in the road.

Looking round, Judas went down from the

road and with immense leaps descended into the depths of a rocky ravine. His clothes blew out with the speed and abruptness of his course, and his hands were extended upwards as though to fly. Lo! now he crept along an abrupt declivity, and suddenly rolled down in a grey ball, rubbing off his skin against the stones, then he jumped up and angrily threatened the mountain with his fist—

"You too, damn you!"

Suddenly he changed his quick movements into a comfortable concentrated dawdling, chose a place by a big stone, and sat down without hurry. He turned himself, as if seeking a comfortable position, laid his hands side by side on the grey stone, and heavily sank his head upon them. And so for an hour or two he sat on, as motionless and grey as the grey stone itself, so still that he deceived even the birds. The walls of the ravine rose before him, and behind, and on every side, cutting a sharp line all round on the blue sky; while everywhere immense grey stones obtruded from the ground, as though there had been here, at some time or other, a shower, and as though its heavy drops had become petrified in endless thought. And the wild, deserted ravine was like a split upturned skull, and every stone in it was like a petrified thought; and there were many of them, and they all kept thinking heavily, boundlessly, stubbornly.

A scorpion, deceived by his quietness, hobbled past, on its tottering legs, close to Judas. He gave a glance at it, and, without lifting his head from the stone, again let both his eyes rest fixedly on something—both motionless, both veiled in a strange whitish turbidness, both as though blind and yet terribly alert. And lo! from out of the ground, the stones, and the clefts the quiet darkness of night began to rise, enveloped the motionless Judas, and crept swiftly up towards the pallid light of the sky. Night was coming on with its thoughts and dreams.

That night Judas did not return to the halting-place. And the disciples, forgetting their thoughts, busied themselves with preparations for their meal, and grumbled at his negligence.

III

ONCE, about mid-day, Jesus and His disciples were walking along a stony and hilly road devoid of shade, and, since they had been more than five hours afoot, Jesus began to complain of weariness. The disciples stopped, and Peter and his friend John spread their cloaks, and those of the other disciples, on the ground, and fastened them above between two high rocks, and so made a sort of tent for Jesus. He lay down in the tent resting from the heat of the sun, while they amused Him with pleasant conversation and jokes. But seeing that even talking fatigued Him, and being themselves but little affected by weariness and the heat, they went some distance off and occupied themselves in various ways. One sought edible roots among the stones on the slope of the mountain, and when he had found them brought them to Jesus; another, climbing up higher and higher, searched musingly for the limits of the blue distance, and failing, climbed up higher on to new sharp-pointed rocks. John found a beautiful little blue lizard among the stones, and smiling brought it quickly with tender hands to Jesus. The lizard looked with its protuberant, mysterious eyes into His, and then crawled quickly with its cold body over His warm hand, and soon swiftly disappeared with tender quivering tail.

But Peter and Philip, not caring about such amusements, occupied themselves in tearing up great stones from the mountain, and hurling them down below, as a test of their strength. The others, attracted by their loud laughter, by degrees gathered round them, and joined in their sport. Exerting their strength, they would tear up from the ground an ancient rock all overgrown, and lifting it high with both hands, hurl it down the slope. Heavily it would strike with a dull thud, and then hesitate for a moment; then irresolutely it would make a first leap, and each time it touched the ground, gathering from it speed and strength, it would become light, furious, all-subservive. Now it no longer leapt, but flew with grinning teeth, and the whistling wind let its dull round mass pass by. Lo! it is on the edge— with a last floating motion the stone would sweep high, and then quietly, with ponderous deliberation, fly downwards in a curve to the invisible bottom of the precipice.

"Now then, another!" cried Peter. His white teeth shone between his black beard and moustache, his mighty chest and arms were bare, and the sullen ancient rocks, dully wondering at the strength which lifted them, obediently, one after another, precipitated themselves into the abyss. Even the frail John threw some moderate-sized stones, and Jesus smiled quietly as He looked at their sport.

"But what are you doing, Judas? Why do you not take part in the game, it seems amusing enough?" asked Thomas, when he found his strange friend motionless behind a great grey stone.

"I have a pain in my chest. Moreover, they have not invited me."

"What need of invitation! At all events I invite you; come! Look what stones Peter throws!"

Judas somehow or other happened to glance sidewards at him, and Thomas became for the first time indistinctly aware that he had two faces. But before he could thoroughly grasp the fact, Judas said in his ordinary tone, at once fawning and mocking—

"There is surely none stronger than Peter? When he shouts all the asses in Jerusalem think that their Messiah has arrived, and lift up their voices too. You have heard them before now, have you not, Thomas?"

Smiling politely, and modestly wrapping his garment round his chest, which was over-

JUDAS ISCARIOT

grown with red curly hairs, Judas stepped into the circle of players.

And since they were all in high good humour, they met him with mirth and loud jokes, and even John condescended to give a smile, when Judas, pretending to groan with the exertion, laid hold of an immense stone. But lo! he lifted it with ease, and threw it, and his blind wide-open eye gave a jerk, and then fixed itself immovably on Peter; while the other eye, cunning and merry, was overflowing with quiet laughter.

"No! you throw again!" said Peter in an offended tone.

And lo! one after the other they kept lifting and throwing gigantic stones, while the disciples looked on in amazement. Peter threw a great stone, and then Judas a still bigger one. Peter, frowning and concentrated, angrily wielded a fragment of rock, and struggling as he lifted it, hurled it down, then Judas, without ceasing to smile, searched for a still larger fragment, and digging his long fingers into it, grasped it, and swinging himself together with it, and paling, sent it into the gulf. When he had thrown his stone, Peter would recoil and so watch its fall; but Judas always bent himself forward, stretched out his long vibrant arms, as though he were going to fly after the stone. Eventually both of them, first Peter then Judas, seized hold of an old grey stone, but neither one nor the other could move it. All red with his exertion, Peter resolutely approached Jesus, and said aloud—

"Lord! I do not wish to be beaten by Judas. Help me to throw this stone."

Jesus answered something in a low voice, and Peter, shrugging his broad shoulders in dissatisfaction, but not daring to make any rejoinder, came back with the words—

"He says: 'But who will help Iscariot?'"

Then glancing at Judas, who, panting with clenched teeth, was still embracing the stubborn stone, he laughed cheerfully—

"Look what an invalid he is! See what our poor sick Judas is doing!"

And even Judas laughed at being so unexpectedly exposed in his deception, and all the others laughed too, and even Thomas allowed his pointed, grey, overhanging moustache to relax into a smile.

And so in friendly chat and laughter they all set out again on the way, and Peter, quite reconciled to his victor, kept from time to time digging him in the ribs, and loudly guffawed—

" There's an invalid for you! "

All of them praised Judas, and acknowledged him victor, and all chatted with him in a friendly manner; but Jesus once again had no word of praise for Judas. He walked silently in front nibbling the grasses, which He plucked. And gradually, one by one, the disciples left off laughing, and went over to Jesus. So that in a short time it came about, that they were all walking ahead in compact body, while Judas—the victor, the strong man—crept on behind choking with dust.

And lo! they stood still, and Jesus laid His hand on Peter's shoulder, while with His other He pointed into the distance, where Jerusalem had just become visible in the smoke. And the broad, strong back of Peter gently accepted that slight sunburnt hand.

For the night they stayed at Bethany at the house of Lazarus. And when all were gathered together for conversation, Judas thought that they would now recall his victory over Peter, and sat down nearer. But the disciples were silent and unusually pensive. Images of the road they had traversed, of the sun, the rocks and the grass, of Christ lying down under the shelter quietly floated through their heads, breathing a soft pensiveness, begetting confused but sweet reveries of an eternal movement under the sun. The wearied body sweetly reposed, and thought was merged in something mystically beautiful and great—and no one recalled Judas!

Judas went out, and then returned. Jesus was discoursing, and His disciples were listening to Him in silence.

Mary sat at His feet motionless as a statue,

and gazed into His face with upturned eyes. John had come quite close, and endeavoured so to sit that his hand touched the garment of the Master, but without disturbing Him. He touched Him and was still. Peter breathed loud and strong, repeating under his breath the words of Jesus.

Iscariot had stopped short on the threshold, and contemptuously letting his gaze pass by the company, he concentrated all its fire on Jesus. And the more he looked the more everything around Him seemed to fade, and to become clothed with darkness and silence, while Jesus alone shone forth with uplifted hand. And then, lo! He was, as it were, raised up into the air, and melted away, as though He consisted of mist floating over a lake, and penetrated by the light of the setting moon, and His soft speech began to sound tenderly somewhere far, far away. And gazing at the wavering phantom, and drinking in the tender melody of the distant dream-like words, Judas gathered his whole soul into his iron fingers, and in its vast darkness silently began building up some colossal scheme. Slowly in the profound darkness he kept lifting up masses, like mountains, and quite easily heaping them one on another: and again he would lift up and again heap them up; and something grew in the darkness, spread noiselessly and burst its bounds. His head felt like a dome, in the impenetrable darkness of which the colossal thing continued to grow, and some one, working on in silence, kept lifting up masses like mountains, and piling them one on another and again lifting up, and so on and on . . . whilst somewhere in the distance the phantom-like words tenderly sounded.

Thus he stood blocking the doorway, huge and black, while Jesus went on talking, and the strong intermittent breathing of Peter repeated His words aloud. But on a sudden Jesus broke off an unfinished sentence, and Peter, as though waking from sleep, cried out exultingly—

"Lord! to Thee are known the words of eternal life!"

But Jesus held His peace, and kept gazing fixedly in one direction. And when they followed His gaze they perceived in the doorway the petrified Judas with gaping mouth and fixed eyes. And, not understanding what was the matter, they laughed. But Matthew, who was learned in the Scriptures, touched Judas on the shoulder, and said in the words of Solomon—

"He that looketh kindly shall be forgiven; but he that is met with in the gates will impede others."

Judas shuddered, and gave a slight cry of fright, and everything about him, his eyes, hands and feet, seemed to start in different directions, as those of an animal which suddenly perceives the eye of man upon him. Jesus went straight to Judas, as though words trembled on His lips, but passed by him through the open, and now unoccupied, door.

In the middle of the night the restless

Thomas came to Judas' bed, and sitting down on his heels, asked—

"Are you weeping, Judas?"

"No! Go away, Thomas."

"Why do you groan, and grind your teeth? Are you ill?"

Judas was silent for a little, and then fretfully there fell from his lips distressful words, fraught with grief and anger—

"Why does not He love me? Why does He love the others? Am I not handsomer, better and stronger than they? Did not I save His life while these ran away like cowardly dogs?"

"My poor friend, you are not quite right. You are not at all good-looking, and your tongue is as disagreeable as your face. You lie and slander continually; how then can you expect Jesus to love you?"

But Judas, stirring heavily in the darkness, continued as though he heard him not—

"Why is He not on the side of Judas, intead of on the side of those who do not love Him? John brought Him a lizard, I would bring Him a poisonous snake. Peter threw stones, I would overthrow a mountain for His sake. But what is a poisonous snake? One has but to draw its fangs, and it will coil round one's neck like a necklace. What is a mountain, which it is possible to dig down with the hands, and to trample with the feet? I would give to Him Judas, the bold, magnificent Judas. But now He will perish, and together with Him will perish Judas."

"You are saying something strange, Judas!"

"A withered fig-tree, which must needs be cut down with the axe, such am I: He said it of me. Why then does He not do it? He dare not, Thomas! I know Him, He fears Judas. He hides from the bold, strong, magnificent Judas. He loves fools, traitors, liars. You are a liar, Thomas; have you never been told so before?"

Thomas was much surprised, and wished to

object, but he thought that Judas was simply railing, and so only shook his head in the darkness. And Judas lamented still more grievously, and groaned and ground his teeth, and it could be heard how his whole huge body heaved under the coverlet.

"What is the matter with Judas? Who has applied fire to his body? He will give his son to the dogs. He will give his daughter to be betrayed by robbers, his bride to harlotry. And yet has not Judas a tender heart? Go away, Thomas; go away, stupid! Leave the strong, bold, magnificent Judas alone!"

IV

Judas had concealed some *denarii*, and the deception was discovered, thanks to Thomas, who had seen by chance how much money had been given to them. It was only too probable that this was not the first time that Judas had committed a theft, and all were enraged. The angry Peter seized Judas by his collar and almost dragged him to Jesus, and the terrified Judas paled but did not resist.

"Master, see! Here he is, the trickster! Here's the thief. You trusted him, and he steals our money. Thief! Scoundrel! If Thou wilt permit, I'll   "

But Jesus held His peace. And attentively regarding him, Peter suddenly turned red, and loosed the hand which held the collar, while Judas shyly rearranged his garment, casting a sidelong glance on Peter, and assuming the downcast look of a repentant criminal.

"So that's how it's to be," angrily said Peter, as he went out, loudly slamming the door. All were dissatisfied, and declared that on no account would they any longer consort with Judas; but John, after some consideration, passed through the door, behind which might be heard the quiet, almost caressing, voice of Jesus. And when in the course of time he returned, he was pale, and his downcast eyes were red as though with recent tears.

"The Master says that Judas may take as much money as he pleases." Peter laughed angrily. John gave him a quick reproachful glance, and suddenly turning red all over, and mingling tears with anger, and delight with tears, loudly exclaimed—

"And no one must reckon how much money Judas receives. He is our brother, and all the money is as much his as ours: if he wants much let him take much, without telling any one, or taking counsel with any.

Judas is our brother, and you have grievously insulted him—so says the Master. Shame on you, brother!"

In the doorway stood Judas, pale and with a distorted smile on his face. With a light movement John went up to him and kissed him three times. After him, glancing round at one another, James, Philip and the others came up shamefacedly; and after each kiss Judas wiped his mouth, but gave a loud smack as though the sound afforded him pleasure. Peter came up last.

"We were all stupid, all blind, Judas. He alone sees, He alone is wise. May I kiss you?"

"Why not? Kiss away!" said Judas as in consent.

Peter kissed him vigorously, and said aloud in his ear—

"But I almost choked you. The others kissed you in the usual way, but I kissed you on the throat. Did it hurt you?"

"A little."

"I will go and tell Him all. I was angry even with Him," said Peter sadly, trying noiselessly to open the door.

"And what are you going to do, Thomas?" asked John severely. He it was who looked after the conduct and the conversation of the disciples.

"I don't know yet. I must consider."

And Thomas thought for long, almost the whole day. The disciples had dispersed to their occupations, and somewhere the other side of the wall, Peter was shouting joyfully —but Thomas was still considering. He would have accomplished this quicker, had not Judas somewhat hindered him by continually following him about with a mocking glance, and now and again asking him in a serious tone—

"Well, Thomas, and how does the matter progress?"

Then Judas brought his money-box, shaking the money, and pretending not to look at Thomas, began to count it—

"Twenty-one, two, three. . . . Look, Thomas, again a bad coin. Oh! what rascals people are, they even give bad money as offerings. Twenty-four . . . and then they will say again that Judas has stolen it . . . twenty-five, twenty-six. . . ."

Thomas approached him resolutely, it was already towards evening, and said—

"He is right, Judas. Let me kiss you."

"Will you? Twenty-nine, thirty. It's no good. I shall steal again. Thirty-one. . . ."

"But how can you steal, when it is neither yours nor another's? You will simply take as much as you want, brother."

"It has taken you a long time to repeat His words! Don't you value time, you clever Thomas?"

"You seem to be laughing at me, brother."

"And consider, are you doing well, my virtuous Thomas, in repeating His words. He said something of His own, but you do not. He really kissed me—you only defiled my mouth. I can still feel your moist lips upon me. It was so disgusting, my good Thomas. Thirty-eight, thirty-nine, forty. Forty *denarii*. Thomas, won't you check the sum?"

"Certainly He is our Master. Why then should we not repeat the words of our Master?"

"Is Judas' collar torn away? Is there now nothing to seize him by? The Master will go out of the house, and Judas will unexpectedly steal three more *denarii*, won't you seize him by the collar?"

"We know now, Judas. We understand."

"Have not all pupils a bad memory? Have not all masters been deceived by their pupils? But the master has only to lift the rod, and the pupils cry out, 'We know, Master!' But the master goes to bed, and the pupils say: 'Did the Master teach us this?' And, so in this case, this morning you called me a thief, this evening you call me brother. What will you call me to-morrow?"

JUDAS ISCARIOT

Judas laughed, and lifting up the heavy rattling money-box with ease, went on—

"When a strong wind blows it raises the dust, and foolish people look at the dust and say: 'Look at the wind!' But it is only dust, my good Thomas, ass's dung trodden underfoot. The dust meets a wall and lies down gently at its foot, but the wind flies farther and farther, my good Thomas."

Judas obligingly pointed over the wall in illustration of his meaning, and laughed again.

"I am glad that you are merry," said Thomas, "but it is a great pity that there is so much malice in your merriment."

"How should not a man be cheerful, who has been so much kissed, and who is so useful? If I had not stolen the three *denarii* would John have known the meaning of delight? Is it not pleasant to be a hook, on which John may hang his damp virtue out to dry, and Thomas his moth-eaten mind?"

"I think that I had better be going."

"But I am only joking, my good Thomas.

I merely wanted to know whether you really wished to kiss the old obnoxious Judas— the thief who stole the three *denarii* and gave them to a harlot."

"To a harlot!" exclaimed Thomas in surprise. "And did you tell the Master of it?"

"Again you doubt, Thomas. Yes, to a harlot. But if you only knew, Thomas, what an unfortunate woman she was. For two days she had had nothing to eat."

"Are you sure of that?" said Thomas in confusion.

"Yes! Of course I am. I myself spent two days with her, and saw that she ate and drank nothing except red wine. She tottered from exhaustion, and I was always falling down with her."

Upon this Thomas got up quickly, and when he had gone a few steps away he flung out at Judas—

"You seem to be possessed of Satan, Judas."

And as he went away, he heard in the approaching twilight how dolefully the heavy money-box rattled in his hands. And Judas seemed to laugh.

But the very next day Thomas was obliged to acknowledge that he had misjudged Judas, so simple, so gentle, and at the same time so serious was Iscariot. He neither grimaced nor made ill-natured jokes, he was neither obsequious nor scurrilous, but quietly and unobtrusively went about his work of catering. He was as active as formerly, as though having not two feet like other people, but a whole dozen of them, and ran noiselessly without that squeaking, sobbing, and laughter like that of a hyena, with which he formerly accompanied his actions. And when Jesus began to speak, he would seat himself quickly in a corner, fold his hands and feet, and look so kindly with his great eyes, that many observed it. He left off speaking evil of people, but rather remained silent, so that even the severe Matthew deemed it possible to praise him, saying in the words of Solomon—

"He that is devoid of wisdom despiseth

his neighbour: but a man of understanding holdeth his peace."

And he lifted up his hand, hinting thereby at Judas' former evil-speaking. In a short time all remarked this change in him, and rejoiced at it: only Jesus looked on him still with the same detached look, although he gave no direct indication of His dislike. And even John, for whom Judas now showed a profound reverence, as the beloved disciple of Jesus, and as his own champion in the matter of the three *denarii*, began to treat him somewhat more kindly, and even sometimes entered into conversation with him.

"What do you think, Judas," said he one day in a condescending manner, "which of us, Peter or I, will be nearest to Christ in His heavenly kingdom?"

Judas meditated, and then answered—

"I suppose that you will."

"But Peter thinks that he will," laughed John.

"No! Peter would scatter all the angels with his shout; you have heard him shout.

Certainly he will quarrel with you, and will endeavour to occupy the first place, as he insists that he, too, loves Jesus. But he is already advanced in years, and you are young; he is heavy on his feet, while you run swiftly; you will enter the first there with Christ? Will you not?"

"Yes, I will not leave Jesus," John agreed.

On the same day Simon Peter referred to Judas the very same question. But fearing that his loud voice would be heard by the others, he led Judas out to the farthest corner behind the house.

"Well then, what is your opinion about it?" he asked anxiously. "You are wise, even the Master praises you for your intellect. And you will speak the truth."

"Of course, you," answered Iscariot without hesitation, and Peter exclaimed with indignation, "I told him so!"

"But of course he will try even there to oust you from the first place."

"Certainly!"

"But what can he do, when you already occupy the place? Won't you be the first to go there with Jesus? You will not leave Him alone? Has He not named you the *Rock?*"

Peter put his hand on Judas' shoulder, and said with warmth: "I tell you, Judas, you are the cleverest of us all. But why are you so sarcastic and malignant? The Master does not like it. Otherwise you might become the beloved disciple, equally with John. But to you neither," and Peter lifted his hand threateningly, "will I yield my place next to Jesus, neither on earth, nor there! Do you hear?"

Thus Judas endeavoured to make himself agreeable to all, but all the while he had in his mind some hidden thoughts. And while he remained ever the same modest, restrained and unobtrusive person, he knew how to say something especially pleasing to each. Thus to Thomas he said—

"The fool believeth every word: but the prudent taketh heed to his paths."

While to Matthew, who suffered somewhat from excess in eating and drinking, and was ashamed of his weakness, he quoted the words of Solomon, the sage whom Matthew held in high estimation—

"The righteous eateth to the satisfying of his soul: but the belly of the wicked shall want."

But his pleasant speeches were rare, which gave them the greater value. For the most part he was silent, attentively listening to what was said, and meditating on something.

When reflecting, Judas had an unpleasant look, ridiculous and at the same time awe-inspiring. As long as his quick, crafty eye was in motion, he seemed simple and good-natured enough, but directly both eyes became fixed in an immovable stare, and the skin on his protuberant forehead became gathered into strange ridges and creases, a distressing surmise would force itself on one, that under that skull some very peculiar thoughts were working. So thoroughly apart, peculiar, and voiceless were the thoughts which encircled Iscariot in the deep silence of secrecy, when he was in one of his reveries, that one would have preferred that he should begin to speak, to move, nay, even to tell lies. For a lie, spoken by a human tongue, had been truth and light compared with that hopelessly deep and unresponsive silence.

"In the dumps again, Judas?" Peter would cry with his clear voice and bright looks, suddenly breaking in upon the sombre silence of Judas' thoughts, and banishing them to some dark corner. "What are you thinking about?"

"Of many things," Iscariot would reply with a quiet smile. And perceiving, apparently, what a bad impression his silence made upon the others, he began more frequently to shun the society of the disciples, and spent much time in solitary walks, or would betake himself to the flat roof and there sit still. And more than once he had startled Thomas, who had unexpectedly stumbled in the darkness against a grey heap, out of which suddenly the hands and feet of Judas started out, and his jeering voice was heard.

But one day, in a specially brusque and strange manner, Judas recalled his former character. This happened on the occasion of the quarrel for the first place in the kingdom of heaven. Peter and John were disputing together, hotly contending each for his own place nearest to Jesus. They reckoned up their services, they measured the degrees of their love for Jesus, they became heated and noisy, and even reviled one another without restraint. Peter roared, all red with anger. John was quiet and pale, with trembling hands and biting speech. Their quarrel had already passed the bounds of decency, and the Master had begun to frown, when Peter looked up by chance on Judas, and laughed self-complacently: John, too, looked at Judas, and also smiled. Each of them recalled what the cunning Judas had said to him. And foretasting the joy of approaching triumph, they, with silent consent, invited Judas to decide the matter.

Peter called out, "Come now, Judas the wise, tell us who will be first near to Jesus, he or I?"

But Judas remained silent, breathing heavily, and with his eyes eagerly questioning the quiet, deep eyes of Jesus.

"Yes," John condescendingly repeated, "tell us who will be first near to Jesus."

Without taking his eyes off Christ, Judas slowly rose, and answered quietly and gravely—

"I."

Jesus slowly let fall His gaze. And quietly striking himself on the breast with a bony finger, Iscariot repeated solemnly and sternly: "I, I shall be near to Jesus!" And he went out. Struck by his insolent freak, the disciples remained silent, only Peter suddenly recalling something, whispered to Thomas in an unexpectedly gentle voice—

"So that is what he is always thinking about! See?"

V

JUST at this time Judas Iscariot took the first definite step towards the Betrayal. He visited the chief priest Annas secretly. He was very roughly received, but that did not disturb him in the least, and he demanded a long private interview. When he found himself alone with the dry, harsh old man, who looked at him with contempt from beneath his heavy overhanging eyelids, he stated that he was an honourable man who had become one of the disciples of Jesus of Nazareth with the sole purpose of exposing the impostor, and handing Him over to the arm of the law.

"But who is this Nazarene?" asked Annas contemptuously, making as though he heard the name of Jesus for the first time.

Judas on his part pretended to believe in

the extraordinary ignorance of the chief priest, and spoke in detail of the preaching of Jesus, of His miracles, of His hatred for the Pharisees and the Temple, of His perpetual infringement of the Law, and eventually of His wish to wrest the power out of the hands of the priesthood, and to set up His own personal kingdom. And so cleverly did he mingle truth with lies, that Annas looked at him more attentively, and lazily remarked: "There are plenty of impostors and madmen in Judah."

"No! He is a dangerous person," Judas hotly contradicted. "He breaks the law. And it were better that one man should perish, rather than the whole people."

Annas, with an approving nod, said—

"But He, apparently, has many disciples."

"Yes, many."

"And they, it seems probable, have a great love for Him?"

"Yes, they say that they love Him, love Him much, more than themselves."

"But if we go about to take Him, will not they stand up for Him? Will they not raise a tumult?"

Judas laughed long and maliciously. "What they? Those cowardly dogs, who run if a man but stoop down to pick up a stone. They indeed!"

"Are they really so bad?" asked Annas coldly.

"But surely it is not the bad who flee from the good, is it not rather the good who flee from the bad? Ha! ha! They are good, and therefore they flee. They are good, and therefore they hide themselves. They are good, and therefore they will appear only in time to bury Jesus. They will lay Him in the tomb themselves, you have only to execute Him."

"But surely they love Him? You yourself said so."

"People always love their teacher, but better dead than alive. While a teacher's alive he may ask them questions which they will find difficult to answer. But when a teacher dies they become teachers themselves, and then others come off badly in turn. Ha! ha!"

Annas looked piercingly at the Traitor, and his lips puckered—which indicated that he was smiling.

"You have been insulted by them. I can see that."

"Can one hide anything from the perspicuity of the astute Annas? You have pierced to the very heart of Judas. Yes, they insulted poor Judas. They said he had stolen from them three *denarii*—as though Judas was not the most honest man in Israel!"

They talked for some time longer about Jesus, and His disciples, and of His pernicious influence on the people of Israel, but on this occasion the crafty, cautious Annas gave no decisive answer. He had long had his eyes on Jesus, and in secret conclave with his own relatives and friends, with the authorities, and the Sadducees, had decided the fate of the Prophet of Galilee. But he did not trust Judas, of whom he had heard as being a bad, untruthful man, and he had no confidence in his flippant trust in the cowardice of the disciples, and of the people. Annas believed in his own power, but he feared bloodshed, feared a serious riot, such as the insubordinate, irascible people of Jerusalem lent itself to so easily; he feared, in fact, the violent intervention of the Roman authorities. Fanned by opposition, fertilized by the red blood of the people, which vivifies everything on which it falls, the heresy would grow stronger, and stifle in its folds Annas, the government, and all his friends. So when a second time Iscariot knocked at his door, Annas was perturbed in spirit and would not admit him. But yet a third and a fourth time Iscariot came to him, persistent as the wind, which beats day and night against the closed door and blows in through its crevices.

"I see that the most astute Annas is afraid

JUDAS ISCARIOT

of something," said Judas when at last he obtained admission to the high priest.

"I am strong enough not to fear anything," Annas answered haughtily. And Iscariot stretched forth his hands and bowed abjectly.

"What do you want?"

"I wish to betray the Nazarene to you."

"We do not want Him."

Judas bowed and waited, humbly fixing his gaze on the high priest.

"Go away."

"But I am bound to return. Am I not, revered Annas?"

"You will not be admitted. Go away!"

But yet again and again Judas called on the aged Annas, and at last was admitted.

Dry and malicious, worried with thought, and silent, he gazed on the Traitor, and as it were counted the hairs on his knotted head. Judas also said nothing, and seemed in his turn to be counting the somewhat sparse grey hairs in the beard of the high priest.

"What? you here again?" the irritated Annas haughtily jerked out, as though spitting upon his head.

"I wish to betray the Nazarene to you."

Both held their peace, and continued to gaze attentively at one another. Iscariot's look was calm; but a quiet malice, dry and cold, began slightly to prick Annas, like the early morning rime of winter.

"How much do you want for your Jesus?"

"How much will you give?"

Annas, with evident enjoyment, insultingly replied: "You are nothing but a band of scoundrels. Thirty pieces—that's what we will give."

And he quietly rejoiced to see how Judas began to squirm and run about—agile and swift as though he had a whole dozen feet, not two.

"Thirty pieces of silver for Jesus!" he cried in a voice of wild madness, most pleasing to Annas. "For Jesus of Nazareth! You wish to buy Jesus for thirty pieces of silver?

And you think that Jesus can be betrayed to you for thirty pieces of silver?" Judas turned quickly to the wall, and laughed in its smooth, white fence, lifting up his long hands. "Do you hear? Thirty pieces of silver! For Jesus!"

With the same quiet pleasure Annas remarked indifferently—

"If you will not deal, go away. We shall find some one to do it cheaper."

And like old-clothes merchants who throw useless rags from hand to hand in the dirty market-place, and shout, and swear and abuse one another, so they embarked in a rabid and fiery bargaining. Intoxicated with a strange rapture, running and turning about, and shouting, Judas ticked off on his fingers the points of Him whom he was selling.

"And the fact that He is kind and heals the sick, is that worth nothing at all in your opinion? Ah, yes! Tell me like an honest man!"

"If you——" began Annas, who was

turning red, as he tried to get in a word, his cold malice quickly warming up under the burning words of Judas, who, however, interrupted him shamelessly—

"That He is young and handsome—like the Narcissus of Sharon, and the Lily of the Valley? What? Is that worth nothing? Perhaps you will say that He is old and useless, and that Judas is trying to dispose of an old bird? Eh?"

"If you——" Annas tried to exclaim; but Judas' stormy speech bore away his senile croak, like down upon the wind.

"Thirty pieces of silver! That will hardly work out to one *obolus* for each drop of blood! Half an *obolus* will not go to a tear! A quarter to a groan. And cries, and convulsions! And for the ceasing of His heart-beats? and the closing of His eyes? Is all this to be given in gratis?" sobbed Iscariot, advancing on to the high priest and enveloping him with insane movement of his hands and fingers, and with intervolved words.

"Includes everything," said Annas in a choking voice.

"And how much will you make out of it yourself? Eh? You wish to rob Judas, to snatch the bit of bread from his children. No, I can't do it. I will go on to the market-place, and shout out: 'Annas has robbed poor Judas. Help!'"

Wearied, and grown quite dizzy, Annas wildly stamped about the floor in his soft slippers, gesticulating: "Be off, be off!"

But Judas on a sudden bowed down, stretching forth his hands submissively—

"But if you really. . . . But why be angry with poor Judas, who only desires his children's good. You also have children, young and handsome."

"We shall find some one else. Be gone!"

"But I—I did not say that I was unwilling to make a reduction. Did I ever say that I was unable to yield. And do I not believe you, that possibly another may come and sell Jesus to fifteen *oboles*—nay, for two —for one.

And bowing lower and lower, wriggling and flattering, Judas submissively consented to the sum offered to him. Annas shamefacedly, with dry, trembling hand, paid him the money, and silently looking round, as though scorched, lifted his head again and again towards the ceiling, and moving his lips rapidly, waited while Judas tested with his teeth all the silver pieces one after another.

"There is now so much bad money about," Judas quickly explained.

"This money was devoted to the Temple by the pious," said Annas, glancing quickly round, and still more quickly turning the ruddy bald nape of his neck to Judas' view.

"But can pious people distinguish between good and bad money? Only rascals can do that."

Judas did not take the money home, but went away outside the city and hid it under a stone. Then he came back again quietly with heavy, slow steps, as a wounded animal creeps slowly to its lair after a sever 'd deadly fight. Only Judas had no lair, here was a house, and in the house he perceived Jesus. Weary and thin, exhausted with continual strife with the Pharisees, who surrounded Him every day in the Temple with a wall of white, shining, scholarly foreheads, He was sitting, leaning His cheek against the rough wall, and apparently fast asleep. Through the open window came in the restless noises of the city. The other side of the wall Peter was hammering, as he put together a new table for the meal, humming the while a quiet Galilean song. But He heard nothing, but slept on peacefully and soundly. And this was He, whom they had bought for thirty pieces of silver.

Coming noiselessly forward, Judas, with the tender touch of a mother, who fears to wake her sick child—with the wonderment of a wild beast as it creeps from its lair suddenly, charmed by the sight of a white flowerlet—he gently touched His soft locks, and then quickly withdrew his hand. Once more he touched Him, and then silently crept out.

"Lord! Lord!" said he.

And going apart he wept long, shrinking, and wriggling, and scratching his bosom with his nails, and gnawing his shoulders. Then suddenly he left off weeping, and gnawing, and gnashing his teeth, and fell into a sombre reverie, inclining his tear-stained face to one side in the attitude of one listening. And so he remained for a long time, doleful, determined, from every one apart, like fate itself.

*   *   *   *   *

Judas surrounded the unhappy Jesus, during those last days of His short life, with quiet love and tender care and caresses. Bashful and timid like a maid in her first love, strangely sensitive and discerning like such an one, he divined the minutest unspoken wishes of Jesus, penetrating to the hidden depth of His feelings, His passing fits of sorrow, and distressing moments of weariness. And whenever Jesus stepped, His foot met something soft, and whenever He turned His gaze, it encountered something pleasing. Formerly Judas had not liked Mary Magdalene and the other women who were near Jesus. He had made rude jests at their expense, and done them little unkindnesses. But now he became their friend, their funny, awkward ally. With deep interest he would talk with them of the charming little idiosyncracies of Jesus, and persistently asking the same questions, he thrust money into their hands, their very palms—and they brought a box of very precious ointment, which Jesus liked so much, and anointed His feet. He himself bought for Jesus, after desperate bargaining, an expensive wine, and then was very angry when Peter drank it nearly all up, with the indifference of a person who looks only to quantity: and in that rocky Jerusalem almost devoid of trees, flowers, and greenery he somehow managed to obtain young spring flowers and green grass, and by means of these same women to give them to Jesus.

For the first time in his life he would take up little children in his arms, finding them somewhere about the courts and streets, and unwillingly kiss them to prevent their crying: and often it would happen that some swarthy urchin with curly hair and dirty little nose, would climb on to the knees of the pensive Jesus, and imperiously demand to be petted. And while they enjoyed themselves together Judas would walk up and down on one side like a severe jailor, who had himself in springtime let in a butterfly to a prisoner, and now pretends to grumble at the breach of discipline.

Of an evening, when together with the darkness alarm took post as sentry by the window, Iscariot would cleverly turn the conversation to Galilee, strange to himself but dear to Jesus, with its still waters and green banks. And he would jog the heavy Peter till his dulled memory awoke, and in clear pictures in which everything was loud, distinct, full of colour, and solid, there arose before his eyes and hearing the dear Galilean life. With eager attention, with half-open mouth in child-like fashion, and with eyes laughing in anticipation, Jesus would listen to his gusty, resonant, cheerful utterance, and sometimes laughed so at his jokes, that it was necessary to interrupt the story for some minutes. But John told tales even better than Peter. There was nothing ludicrous, nor startling, about his stories, but everything became so pensive, unusual, and beautiful, that tears would appear in Jesus' eyes, and He would sigh softly, while Judas nudged Mary Magdalene and excitedly whispered to her—

"What a narrator he is! Do you hear?"

"Yes, certainly."

"No, be more attentive. You women never make good listeners."

Then they would all quietly disperse to bed, and Jesus would kiss His thanks to John, and stroke kindly the shoulder of the tall Peter.

And without envy, but with a condescending contempt, Judas would witness these caresses. Of what importance were these tales, and kisses, and sighs compared with what he, Judas Iscariot, the red-haired, misshapen Judas, begotten among the rocks, could tell them if he chose.

VI

With one hand betraying Jesus, Judas tried hard with the other to frustrate his own plans. He did not indeed endeavour to dissuade Jesus from the last dangerous journey to Jerusalem, as did the women; he even inclined rather to the side of the relatives of Jesus, and of those amongst His disciples who looked for a victory over Jerusalem as indispensable to the full triumph of His cause. But he kept continually, and obstinately, warning them of the danger, and in lively colours depicted the threatening hatred of the Pharisees for Jesus, and their readiness to commit any crime if, either secretly or openly, they might make an end of the Prophet of Galilee. Each day and every hour he kept talking of this, and there was not one of the believers before whom Judas had not stood with uplifted finger and uttered this serious warning—

"We must look after Jesus. We must

stand up for Jesus, when He comes to that hour."

But whether it was the unlimited faith which the disciples had in the miracle-working power of their Master, or the consciousness of their own uprightness, or whether it was simply blindness, the alarming words of Judas were met with a smile, and his continual advice provoked only a grumble. When Judas procured, somewhere or other, two swords, and brought them, only Peter approved of them, and gave Judas his meed of praise, while the others complained—

"Are we soldiers that we should be made to gird on swords? Is Jesus a captain of the host, and not a prophet?"

"But if they go about to kill Him?"

"They will not dare when they perceive how all the people follow Him."

"But if they should dare! What then?"

John replied disdainfully—

"One would think, Judas, that you were the only one who loved Jesus!"

And eagerly seizing hold of these words, and not in the least offended, Judas began to question impatiently and hotly, with stern insistency—

"But you love Him, don't you?"

And there was not one of the believers who came to Jesus whom he did not ask more than once: "Do you love Him? Dearly love Him?"

And all answered that they loved Him.

He used often to converse with Thomas, and holding up his dry, hooked fore-finger, with its long, dirty nail, in warning, would mysteriously say—

"Look here, Thomas, the terrible hour is drawing near. Are you prepared for it? Why did you not take the sword I brought you?"

Thomas would reply with deliberation—

"We are men not accustomed to the use of arms. If we were to join issue with the Roman soldiery, they would kill us all one after the other. Besides, you brought only two swords, and what could one do with only two?"

"We could get more. We could take them from the Roman soldiers," Judas impatiently objected, and even the serious Thomas smiled through his overhanging moustache.

"Ah! Judas! Judas! But where did you get these? They are like Roman swords."

"I stole them. I could have stolen more, only some one gave the alarm, and I fled."

Thomas considered a little, then said sorrowfully—

"Again you acted ill, Judas. Why do you steal?"

"There is no such thing as property."

"No, but to-morrow they will ask the soldiers: 'Where are your swords?' And when they cannot find them they will be punished though innocent."

The consequence was, that after the death of Jesus the disciples recalled these conversations of Judas, and determined that he had

JUDAS ISCARIOT

wished to destroy them, together with the Master, by inveigling them into an unequal and murderous conflict. And once again they cursed the hated name of Judas Iscariot the Traitor.

But the angry Judas after each conversation would go to the women and weep. They heard him gladly. The tender womanly element, that there was in his love for Jesus, drew him near to them, and made him simple, comprehensible, and even handsome in their eyes; although, as before, a certain amount of disdain was perceptible in his attitude towards them.

"Are they men?" he would bitterly complain of the disciples, fixing his blind, motionless eye confidingly on Mary Magdalene. "They are not men. They have not an *oboles*' worth of blood in their veins!"

"But then you always are speaking ill of others," Mary objected.

"Have I ever?" said Judas in surprise. "Oh yes, I have indeed spoken ill of them, but is there not room for improvement in them? Ah! Mary, silly Mary, why are you not a man, to carry a sword?"

"It is so heavy, I could not lift it!" said Mary smilingly.

"But you will lift it, when men are too worthless. Did you give Jesus the lily that I found on the mountain. I got up early to find it, and this morning the sun was so beautiful, Mary! Was He pleased with it? Did He smile?"

"Yes, He was pleased. He said that its smell reminded Him of Galilee."

"But surely, you did not tell Him that it was Judas—Judas Iscariot—who got it for Him?"

"Why, you asked me not to tell Him."

"Yes, certainly, quite right," said Judas, with a sigh. "You might have let it out, though, women are such chatterers. But you did not let it out; no, you were firm. You are a good woman, Mary. You know that I have a wife somewhere. Now I should be glad to see her again, perhaps she is not a bad woman either. I don't know. She said, 'Judas was a liar and malignant,' so I left her. But she may be a good woman. Do you know?"

"How should I know, when I have never seen your wife."

"True, true, Mary! But what think you, is thirty pieces of silver a large sum? Is it not rather a small one?"

"I should say a small one."

"Certainly, certainly. How much did you get when you were a harlot, five pieces of silver or ten? You were an expensive one, were you not?"

Mary Magdalene blushed, and dropped her head till her luxuriant golden hair completely covered her face, so that nothing but her round white chin was visible.

"How bad you are, Judas; I want to forget about that, and you remind me of it!"

"No, Mary, you must not forget that, why should you? Let others forget that you were a harlot, but you must remember. It is the others who should forget as soon as possible, but you should not; why should you?"

"But it was a sin!"

"He fears who never committed a sin, but he who has committed it, what has he to fear? Do the dead fear death; is it not rather the living? No, the dead laugh at the living and their fears."

Thus by the hour would they sit and talk in friendly guise, he—already old, dried-up and misshapen, with his bulbous head and monstrous double-sided face; she—young, modest, tender, and charmed with life as with a story or a dream.

But time rolled by unconcernedly, while the thirty pieces of silver lay under the stone, and the terrible day of the Betrayal drew inevitably near. Already Jesus had ridden into Jerusalem on the ass's back, and the people, strewing their garments in the way, had greeted Him with enthusiastic cries of "Osanna! Osanna! He that cometh in the name of the Lord!"

So great was the exultation, so unrestrainedly did their loving cries rend the skies, that Jesus wept, but His disciples proudly said—

"Is not this the Son of God with us?"

And themselves cried out with enthusiasm—

"Osanna! Osanna! He that cometh in the name of the Lord!"

That evening it was long before they went to bed, recalling the enthusiastic and joyful reception. Peter was like a madman, as though possessed by the demon of merriment and pride. He shouted, drowning all voices with his leonine roar; he laughed, hurling his laughter at their heads, like great round stones; he kept kissing John and James, and even gave a kiss to Judas. He noisily confessed that he had had great fears for Jesus, but that he feared nothing now, that he had seen the love of the people for Him.

Swiftly moving his vivid, watchful eye, Judas glanced in surprise from side to side. He meditated, and then again listened, and looked. Then he took Thomas aside, and pinning him, as it were, to the wall with his keen gaze, he asked in doubt and fear, but with a certain confused hopefulness—

"Thomas! But what if He is right? What if He be founded upon a rock, and we upon sand? What then?"

"Of whom are you speaking?"

"How, then, would it be with Judas Iscariot? Then I should be obliged to strangle Him in order to do right. Who is deceiving Judas? You or himself? Who is deceiving Judas? Who?"

"I don't understand you, Judas. You speak very unintelligibly. Who is deceiving Judas? Who is right?"

And Judas nodded his head and repeated like an echo—

"Who is deceiving Judas? Who?"

And the next day, in the way in which Judas raised his hand with thumb bent back,[1] and by the way in which he looked at

---

[1] Does our author refer to the Roman sign of disapprobation, *vertere*, or *convertere*, *pollicem* ?—Tr.

Thomas, the same strange question was implied—

"Who is deceiving Judas? Who is right?"

And still more surprised, and even alarmed, was Thomas, when suddenly in the night he heard the loud, apparently glad voice of Judas—

"Then Judas Iscariot will be no more. Then Jesus will be no more. Then there will be Thomas, the stupid Thomas! Did you ever wish to take the earth and lift it? And then, possibly hurl it away."

"That's impossible. What are you talking about, Judas?"

"It's quite possible," said Iscariot with conviction, "and we will lift it up some day when you are asleep, stupid Thomas. Go to sleep. I'm enjoying myself. When you sleep your nose plays the Galilean pipe. Sleep!"

But now the believers were already dispersed about Jerusalem, hiding in houses and behind walls, and the faces of those that met them looked mysterious. The exultation had died down. Confused reports of danger found their way in; Peter, with gloomy countenance, tested the sword given to him by Judas, and the face of the Master became even more melancholy and stern. So swiftly the time passed, and inevitably approached the terrible day of the Betrayal. Lo! the Last Supper was over, full of grief and confused dread, and already had the obscure words of Jesus sounded concerning some one who should betray Him.

"You know who will betray Him?" asked Thomas, looking at Judas with his straightforward, clear, almost transparent eyes.

"Yes, I know," Judas replied harshly and decidedly. "You, Thomas, will betray Him. But He Himself does not believe what He says! It is full time! Why does He not call to Him the strong, magnificent Judas?"

No longer by days, but by short fleeting hours, was the inevitable time to be measured.

It was evening; and evening stillness and long shadows lay upon the ground—the first sharp darts of the coming night of mighty contest—when a harsh, sorrowful voice was heard. It said—

"Dost Thou know whither I go, Lord? I go to betray Thee into the hands of Thine enemies."

And there was a long silence, evening stillness, and swift black shadows.

"Thou art silent, Lord? Thou commandest me to go?"

And again silence.

"Allow me to remain. But perhaps Thou canst not? Or darest not? Or willest not?"

And again silence, stupendous, like the eyes of eternity.

"But indeed Thou knowest that I love Thee, Thou knowest all things. Why lookest Thou thus at Judas? Great is the mystery of Thy beautiful eyes, but is mine less? Order me to remain! But Thou art silent, Thou art ever silent. Lord, Lord, is it for this that in grief and pains have I sought Thee all my life, sought and found! Free me! Remove the weight, it is heavier than even mountains of lead. Dost Thou hear how the bosom of Judas Iscariot is cracking under it?"

And the last silence was abysmal, like the last glance of eternity.

"I go."

But the evening stillness woke not up, neither uttered cry nor plaint, nor did its subtle air vibrate with the slightest tinkle—so soft was the fall of the retreating steps. They sounded for a time, and then were silent. And the evening stillness became pensive, stretched itself out in long shadows, and then became dark;—and suddenly night coming to meet it, all asigh with the rustle of sadly brushed-up leaves, heaved a last sigh and was still.

There was bustle, a jostle, a rattle of other voices, as though some one had untied a bag of lively resonant voices, and they were falling out on to the ground, by one and two, and whole heaps. It was the disciples talking. And drowning them all, reverberating from the trees and walls, and tripping up over itself, thundered the determined, powerful voice of Peter—he was swearing that never would he desert his Master.

"Lord," said he, half in anger, half in grief: "Lord! I am ready to go with Thee to prison and to death."

And quietly, like the soft echo of some one's retiring footsteps, came the inexorable answer—

"I tell thee, Peter, the cock will not crow this day before thou dost deny Me thrice."

VII

THE moon had already risen when Jesus set out for the Mount of Olives, where He spent the whole of His last night. But for some unknown reason He delayed, and the disciples, who were ready to start, were hastening Him, when He suddenly said—

"He who hath a wallet let him take it, and also a purse; and he who hath not, let him sell his garments and buy a sword. For I say unto you that in Me must the Scriptures be fulfilled: 'And He was numbered among the transgressors.'"

The disciples were astonished and looked at one another in confusion. But Peter answered—

"Lord! here are two swords."

He looked searchingly into their kindly faces, and bowing His head, said quietly: "It is enough."

Their footfalls resounded loudly in the narrow streets as they walked—and the disciples were afraid of the sound of their own steps; their black shadows stood out against the white moon-lit wall—and they were afraid of their own shadows. Thus in silence they went through the sleeping Jerusalem, and then out beyond the gates, and into the deep ravine full of mysteriously motionless shadows; the brook Kedron came into view. Now everything frightened them. The gentle purling and splashing of the water against the stones seemed to them like the voices of people surreptitiously approaching them. The monstrous shadows of rocks and trees, which barred the road, frightened them with their diapering of light and shade, and the motionlessness of night seemed to them all movement. But the higher they ascended the hill, and the nearer they approached the garden of Gethsemane, where they had passed so many nights in safety and peace, the bolder they became.

Now and then they looked round at Jerusalem, which they had left behind them, all white in the moonlight, and talked together of the fear that was past; and those who were walking behind heard disjointedly the quiet words of Jesus. He was saying that they would all forsake Him.

They stopped near the entrance of the garden. The greater part of them remained on the same spot, and began with quiet talk to dispose themselves to sleep, spreading out their cloaks in the transparent lacery of the shadows and moonlight. But Jesus, wearied with anxiety, and His four nearest disciples, went farther into the depths of the garden.

There they sat down on the ground, which had not yet cooled from the heat of the day, and while Jesus remained silent Peter and John lazily exchanged words, almost devoid of meaning. Yawning with weariness they talked of the coldness of the night, and of how that meat was dear in Jerusalem, and fish quite unprocurable. They endeavoured to determine in exact figures the number of pilgrims that were gathered together in the city for the Feast, and Peter, drawling out his words with a loud yawn, said that there were twenty thousand, while John and his brother James affirmed equally lazily that there were not more than ten thousand.

Suddenly Jesus got up.

"My soul is exceedingly sorrowful unto death. Abide ye here and watch," said He, as with hasty steps He withdrew into the thicket, and was quickly lost in its motionless shadows and light.

"Where is He gone?" said John, lifting himself up on his elbow.

Peter turned his head in the direction of His retreating form and said in weary tones—

"I know not!"

And yawning once more aloud he threw himself on his back, and lay still. Still too lay the others, and the deep sleep of healthy fatigue claimed their motionless bodies for its own. Peter, sunk in a heavy slumber, saw indistinctly something white bend over him, and some one's voice sounded and then was silent, leaving behind it no impression on his drowsy consciousness—

"Simon, sleepest thou?"

Again he fell asleep, and again a gentle voice just touched his hearing and ceased, leaving no trace behind it—

"What, could ye not watch with Me one hour?"

"Ah, Lord, if only Thou knewest how sleepy I am!" thought he, half asleep, but it seemed to him that he spoke it out aloud. And once more he fell asleep, and a considerable space of time seemed to have elapsed, when suddenly the figure of Jesus rose up near to him, and a loud voice instantaneously brought him and the others to their senses—

"Are ye still sleeping and resting? Verily the hour is come, behold the Son of Man is being betrayed into the hands of sinners."

The disciples leapt quickly to their feet, seizing their cloaks in confusion, and shivering with the effects of sudden awakening.

Through the density of the trees, which they lit up with the flitting flames of torches, a crowd of soldiers and servitors of the Temple was approaching with shouts and stamping, and the clash of arms, and the crackling of broken branches. On the other side the disciples were running up trembling with cold and with sleepy, terrified faces, and not yet grasping the situation, were hastily inquiring—

"What is it? Who are these people with torches?"

The pale Thomas, with his straight moustache now bent down, and his teeth chattering with the cold, said to Peter—

"Apparently they are come after us."

The crowd of soldiers surrounded them, and the alarming smoky light of the torches drove out the calm sheen of the moon to somewhere outwards and upwards. Judas moved hurriedly in front of the soldiers, and rolling his one vivid eye was searching for Jesus with piercing glance. He found Him, and for an instant stood still with his gaze fixed on the tall slight figure of Jesus, and then quickly whispered to the servitors—

"Whomsoever I kiss, that is He. Seize Him, and lead Him away cautiously. Cautiously—do you hear?"

Then quickly he approached Jesus, who was awaiting him in silence, and plunged his direct sharp glance, like a knife, into His quiet darkening eyes.

"Hail, Rabbi!" said he aloud, putting a strange and threatening meaning into the words of ordinary salutation.

But Jesus held His peace, and the disciples glanced with horror on the Traitor, being unable to understand how the soul of a man could harbour so much wickedness.

In one swift glance Iscariot took in their disordered ranks; he observed their torpid attitude, on the verge of the loudly chattering shudder of terror; he observed their paleness, their meaningless smiles, the impotent movements of their hands, as though attached to the forearms with iron wire; and there was kindled in his heart a deathlike sorrow, like that experienced a little before by Christ.

Drawn out into a hundred vibrating, sobbing strings he rushed quickly to Jesus, and tenderly kissed His cold neck—so gently, so tenderly, with such agonized love and grief, that had Jesus been a flowerlet on a slender little stalk, he would not have shaken Him with that kiss, nor have spilt the pearly drops of dew from the pure petals.

"Judas!" said Jesus, and with the lifting of His gaze He lit up that monstrous heap of watchful shadows which formed the soul of Iscariot, but could not penetrate its bottomless depths, "Judas! betrayest thou the Son of Man with a kiss?"

And He saw how the whole of that monstrous chaos shuddered and came into motion. Silent and stern, as death in its austere greatness, stood Judas Iscariot, while within he was all agroan, and roaring and howling with a thousand tumultuous and fiery voices.

"Yes! with the kiss of love we betray Thee! with the kiss of love we betray Thee to insult, to torture, to death! With the voice of love we call out the executioners from their dark holes, we set up a cross, and high above the dark earth we lift up upon the cross Love crucified by love."

Judas stood thus, silent and cold as death, but the noise and cries which arose round Jesus answered the cry of his soul. With the rude indecision of an armed force, with the clumsiness of an ill-defined purpose, the soldiers had seized Him by the hands and were dragging Him some whither—taking their own indecision for reluctance, and their very fear for mockery and derision of others. Like a flock of terrified lambs the disciples crowded together, preventing none, but hindering all, even themselves; and only a few determined to go, and act independently of the others. Simon Peter, pushed about on every side, with difficulty drew his sword as though he had lost all his strength, and brought it down with a weak slanting blow on the head of one of the servitors, but did no harm. Jesus, observing this, ordered him to throw away the useless weapon, and it fell under foot with a dull sound, and so evidently had it lost its sharpness and killing power that it did not enter into the head of any one to pick it up. So it rolled about under foot, until several days afterwards it was found on the same spot by some children at play, who made a toy of it.

The soldiers kept dispersing the disciples, but they gathered together again and stupidly got under the soldiers' feet, and this went on so long that at last a contemptuous rage mastered the soldiery. One of them with frowning brow went up to the shouting John; another rudely pushed from his shoulder the hand of Thomas, who was arguing with him about something or other, and shook a big fist right in front of his straightforward, transparent eyes. John fled, and Thomas and

James fled, and all the disciples, as many as were present, forsook Jesus and fled. Losing their cloaks, knocking themselves against the trees, tripping up against stones and falling, they fled to the hills terror-driven, while in the stillness of the moonlight night the ground rumbled loudly beneath the tramp of many feet. Some one, whose name did not transpire, just risen from his bed (for he was covered only with a blanket), rushed excitedly into the crowd of soldiers and servants. When they tried to stop him, and seized hold of his blanket, he gave a cry of terror, and took to flight like the others, leaving his garment in the hands of the soldiers. And so stark-naked he ran with desperate leaps, and his naked body glistened strangely in the moonlight.

When they led Jesus away Peter, who had hidden himself behind some trees, came out and followed the Master at a distance. Seeing a man in front of him walking in silence he thought that it was John, and called to him softly—

"Is that you, John?"

"Is that you, Peter?" he replied, stopping, and by his voice Peter recognized him as the Traitor. "Why did you not run away with the rest, Peter?"

Peter stopped, and uttered with loathing the words—

"Get thee from me, satan!"

Judas smiled, and taking no further notice of Peter went on to where the torches gave a smoky light, and the jingle of arms was mingled with the measured tramp of feet. Peter also followed them cautiously, and so they entered almost simultaneously the courtyard of the high priest's palace, and pushed in among the crowd of servants who were warming themselves at the fires.

As Judas was grimly warming his bony hands over the fire, he heard Peter somewhere behind him saying—

"No, I know Him not."

And then evidently they insisted that he was one of Jesus' disciples, since Peter repeated still louder—

"No, indeed! I understand not what you say!"

Without looking round, and involuntarily smiling, Judas gave an affirmative nod with his head, and murmured—

"That's right, Peter! Don't yield your place next to Him to any one!"

But he did not see how the terrified Peter left the court, so as to be seen no more.

From that evening, till the death of Jesus, Judas did not see any of the disciples near Him again; but in the midst of that crowd were only they two, inseparable till death, strangely bound together by a community of suffering. He, who was betrayed to ignominy and torture, and he who betrayed Him. Of one and the same cup of suffering, like brothers, they both were drinking, the Betrayed and the Betrayer, and the fiery liquid burnt equally the clean and the unclean lips.

Gazing fixedly at the wood-fire, which imparted a feeling of warmth to his eyes, stretching out his long, shaking hands to the flame, his hands and feet forming a confused outline in the trembling light and shade, Iscariot kept mumbling in hoarse complaint—

"How cold! My God, how cold it is!"

So, when the fishermen go away at night leaving an expiring fire of drift-wood upon the shore, from the dark depth of the sea might something creep forth, crawl up towards the fire, look at it with wild intentness, and dragging all its limbs up to it, mutter in hoarse complaint—

"How cold! My God, how cold it is!"

Suddenly Judas heard behind him a burst of loud voices, the cries and laughter of the soldiers full of the usual sleepy, greedy malice; and lashes, short frequent strokes upon a living body. He turned round, a momentary anguish running through his whole body—his very bones. They were scourging Jesus.

Is it come to that?

He had seen how the soldiers had led Jesus away with them to their guardroom. The night was already nearly over, the fires had sunk down and were covered with ashes, but from the guardroom was still borne the sound of muffled cries, laughter, and invectives. They were scourging Jesus.

As one who has lost his way Iscariot ran nimbly about the empty courtyard, stopped in his course, lifted his head and ran on again, and was surprised when he came into collision with heaps of embers, or with the walls.

Then he clung to the wall of the guardroom, stretched himself out to his full height, and glued himself to the window and the crevices of the door, eagerly examining what they were doing. He saw a confined stuffy room, dirty, like all guardrooms in the world, with bespitten floor, and walls as greasy and stained as though they had been trodden and rolled upon. And he saw the Man whom they were scourging. They struck Him on the face and head, and tossed Him about like a soft bundle from one end of the room to the other. And since He neither cried out nor resisted, after looking intently, it actually appeared at moments as though it was not a living human being, but a soft effigy without bones or blood. It bent itself strangely like a doll, and in falling, knocking its head against the stone floor it did not give the impression of a hard substance striking against a hard substance, but of something soft and devoid of feeling. And when one looked long, it became like some strange, endless game—and sometimes it became almost a complete illusion.

After one hard kick the man or effigy fell slowly on its knees before a sitting soldier, he in his turn knocked it away, and turning over it dropped down before the next, and so on and on. A loud guffaw arose, and Judas also smiled—as though the strong hand of some one with iron fingers had torn his mouth asunder. It was the mouth of Judas that was deceived.

Night dragged on, and the fires were still smouldering. Judas threw himself from the wall, and crawled to one of the fires, poked up the ashes, made it up, and although he no longer felt the cold he stretched his slightly trembling hands over the flames, and began to mutter dolefully—

"Ah! how painful, my Son, my Son; how painful!"

Then he went again to the window, which was gleaming yellow with a dull light between the thick grating, and once more began to watch them scourging Jesus. Once before the very eyes of Judas appeared His swarthy countenance, now marred out of human semblance, and covered with a forest of dishevelled hair. Then some one's hand plunged into those locks, threw the Man down, and rhythmically turning His head from one side to the other, began to wipe the filthy floor with His face. Right under the window a soldier was sleeping, his open mouth revealing his glittering white teeth; and some one's broad back, with naked, brawny neck, barred the window, so that nothing more could be seen. And suddenly the noise ceased.

"What's that? Why are they silent? Have they suddenly divined the truth?"

Momentarily the whole head of Judas, in

all its parts, was filled with the rumbling, shouting and roaring of a thousand maddened thoughts! Had they divined? They understood that this was the very best of men—it was so simple, so clear! Lo! He is coming out, and behind Him they were abjectly crawling. Yes, He is coming here, to Judas, coming out a victor, a hero, arbiter of the truth, a god. . . .

"Who is deceiving Judas? Who is right?"

But no. Once more noise and shouting. They are scourging Him again. They do not understand, they have not guessed, they are beating Him harder, more cruelly than ever. The fires burn out, covered with ashes, and the smoke above them is as transparently blue as the air, and the sky as bright as the moon. It was the day coming on.

"What is day?" asks Judas.

And lo! everything began to glow, to scintillate, to grow young again, and the smoke above was no longer blue, but rose-coloured. It was the sun rising.

"What is the sun?" asks Judas.

VIII

They pointed the finger at Judas, and some in contempt, others with hatred and fear, said—

" Look, that is Judas the Traitor! "

This already began to be the opprobrious title, to which he had doomed himself throughout the ages. Thousands of years may pass, nation may supplant nation, and still the air will resound with the words, uttered with contempt and fear by good and bad alike—

" Judas the Traitor! "

But he listened imperturbably to what was said of him, dominated by a feeling of burning, all-subduing curiosity. Ever since the morning when they led forth Jesus from the guardroom, after scourging Him, Judas had followed Him, strangely enough feeling neither grief nor pain nor joy—only an unconquerable desire to see and hear everything. Though he had had no sleep the whole night, his body felt light : when he was crushed and prevented from advancing, he elbowed his way through the crowd and adroitly wormed himself into the front place; and not for a moment did his vivid quick eye remain at rest. At the examination of Jesus before Caiaphas, in order not to lose a word, he hollowed his hand round his ear, and nodded his head in affirmation, murmuring—

" Just so! Thou hearest, Jesus? "

But he was a prisoner, like a fly tied to a thread, which buzzing flies hither and thither; but cannot for one moment free itself from the tractable, but unyielding thread.

Certain stony thoughts lay at the back of his head, and to these he was firmly bound; he knew not, as it were, what these thoughts were; he did not wish to stir them up, but he felt them continually. At times they would come to him all of a sudden, oppress him more and more, and begin to crush him with their unimaginable weight, as though the vault of a rocky cavern were slowly and terribly descending upon his head.

Then he would grip his heart with his hand, and strive to set his whole body in motion, as though he were perished with cold, and hasten to shift his eyes to a fresh place, and again to another. When they led Jesus away from Caiaphas he met His weary eyes quite close, and, somehow or other, unconsciously he gave Him several friendly nods.

"I am here, my Son, I am here," he muttered hurriedly, and maliciously gave a shove in the back to some gaper who stood in his way.

And now, in a huge shouting crowd, they all moved on to Pilate for the last examination and trial, and with the same insupportable curiosity Judas searched the faces of the ever swelling multitude. Many were quite unknown to him, Judas had never seen them before, but some were there who had cried,

"Osanna!" to Jesus, and at each step the number of them seemed to increase.

"Well, well!" thought Judas, and his head spun round as if he were drunk, "the worst is over. Directly they will be crying: 'He is ours, He is Jesus! what are you about?' and all will understand, and "

But the believers walked in silence. Some hypocritically smiled, as who should say: "The affair is none of ours!" Others spoke with constraint, but their low voices were drowned in the rumbling of movement, and the loud delirious shouts of His enemies.

And Judas felt better again. Suddenly he noticed Thomas cautiously slipping through the crowd not far off, and struck by a sudden thought he was about to go up to him. At the sight of the traitor Thomas was frightened, and tried to hide himself; but in a little narrow street, between two walls, Judas overtook him.

"Thomas, wait a bit!"

Thomas stopped, and stretching both hands

out in front of him solemnly pronounced the words—

"Avaunt, Satan!"

Iscariot made an impatient movement of the hands.

"What a fool you are, Thomas! I thought that you had more sense than the others. Satan indeed! That requires proof."

Letting his hands fall, Thomas asked in surprise—

"But did not you betray the Master? I myself saw you bring the soldiers, and point Him out to them. If this is not treachery, I should like to know what is!"

"Never mind that," hurriedly said Judas. "Listen, there are many of you here. You must all gather together, and loudly demand: 'Give up Jesus. He is ours!' They will not refuse you, they dare not. They themselves will understand."

"What do you mean! What are you thinking about!" said Thomas, with a decisive wave of his hands. "Have you not seen what a number of armed soldiers and servants of the Temple there are here. Moreover, the trial has not yet taken place, and we must not interfere with the court. Surely he understands that Jesus is innocent, and will order His release without delay."

"You, then, think so too," said Judas thoughtfully. "Thomas, Thomas, what if it be the truth? What then? Who is right? Who has deceived Judas?"

"We were talking all last night, and came to the conclusion that the court cannot condemn the innocent. But if it does, why then——"

"What then!"

"Why, then it is no court. And it will be the worse for them when they have to give an account before the real Judge."

"Before the real! Is there any 'real' left?" sneered Judas.

"And all of our party cursed you; but since you say that you were not the traitor, I think you ought to be tried."

Judas did not want to hear him out; but turned right about, and hurried down the street in the wake of the retreating crowd. He soon, however, slackened his pace, mindful of the fact that a crowd always travels slowly, and that a single pedestrian will inevitably overtake it.

When Pilate led Jesus out from his palace, and set Him before the people, Judas, crushed against a column by the heavy backs of the soldiers, furiously turning his head about to see something between two shining helmets, suddenly felt clearly that the worst was over. He saw Jesus in the sunshine, high above the heads of the crowd, blood-stained, pale with a crown of thorns, the sharp spikes of which pressed into His forehead.

He stood on the edge of an elevation, visible from His head to His small, sunburnt feet, and waited so calmly, was so serene in His immaculate purity, that only a blind man, who sees not the very sun, could fail to perceive it, only a madman would not understand it. And the people held their peace—it was so still, that Judas heard the breathing of the soldier in front of him, and how that at each breath a strap creaked somewhere about his body.

"Yes, it will soon be over! They will understand immediately," thought Judas, and suddenly something strange, like the dazzling joy of falling from a giddy height into a blue sparkling abyss, arrested his heart-beats.

Contemptuously drawing his lips down to his rounded well-shaven chin, Pilate flung to the crowd the dry curt words—as one throws bones to a pack of hungry hounds—thinking to cheat their longing for fresh blood and living, palpitating flesh—

"You have brought this Man before me as a corrupter of the people, and behold I have examined Him before you, and I find this Man guiltless of that of which you accuse him. . . ."

Judas closed his eyes. He was waiting.

All the people began to shout, to sob, to howl with a thousand voices of wild beasts and men—

"Put Him to death! Crucify Him! Crucify Him!" And as though in self-mockery, as though wishing in one moment to plumb the very depths of all possible degradation, madness and shame, the crowd cries out, sobs, and demands with a thousand voices of wild beasts and men.

"Release unto us Barabbas! But crucify Him! Crucify Him!"

But the Roman had evidently not yet said his last word. Over his proud, shaven countenance there passed convulsions of disgust and anger. He understood! He has understood all along! He speaks quietly to his attendants, but his voice is not heard in the roar of the crowd. What does he say? Is he ordering them to bring swords, and to smite those maniacs.

"Bring water."

"Water? What water? What for?"

Ah, lo! he washes his hands. Why does he wash his clean white hands all adorned with rings? He lifts them and cries angrily to the people, whom surprise holds in silence—

"I am innocent of the blood of this Just Person. See ye to it."

While the water is still dripping from his fingers on to the marble pavement, something soft prostrates itself at his feet, and sharp, burning lips kiss his hand, which he is powerless to withdraw, glue themselves to it like tentacles, almost bite and draw blood. He looks down in disgust and fear, and sees a great squirming body, a strangely twofold face, and two immense eyes so strangely diverse from one another that, as it were, not one being but a number of them clung to his hands and feet. He heard a broken, burning whisper—

"O wise and noble . . . wise and noble."

And with such a truly satanic joy did that wild face blaze, that with a cry Pilate kicked him away, and Judas fell backwards. And there he lay upon the stone flags like an overthrown demon, still stretching out his hand to the departing Pilate, and crying as one passionately enamoured—

"O wise, O wise and noble. . . ."

Then he gathered himself up with agility, and ran away accompanied by the laughter of the soldiery. Evidently there was yet hope. When they come to see the cross, and the nails then they will understand, and then. . . . What then? He catches sight of the panic-stricken Thomas in passing, and for some reason or other reassuringly nods to him; he overtakes Jesus being led to execution. The walking is difficult, small stones roll under the feet, and suddenly Judas feels that he is tired. He gives himself up wholly to the trouble of deciding where best to plant his feet, he looks dully around, and sees Mary Magdalene weeping, and a number of women weeping—hair dishevelled, eyes red, lips distorted—all the excessive grief of a tender woman's soul when submitted to outrage.

JUDAS ISCARIOT   127

Suddenly he revives, and seizing the moment, runs up to Jesus—

"I go with Thee," he hurriedly whispers.

The soldiers drive him away with blows of their whips, and squirming so as to avoid the blows, and showing his teeth at the soldiers, he explains hurriedly—

"I go with Thee. Thither. Thou understandest whither."

He wipes the blood from his face, shakes his fist at one of the soldiers, who turns round and smiles, and points him out to the others. Then he looks for Thomas, but neither he nor any of the disciples are in the crowd that accompanies Jesus. Again he is conscious of fatigue, and drags one foot with difficulty after the other, as he attentively looks out for the sharp, white, scattered pebbles.

When the hammer was uplifted to nail Jesus' left hand to the tree, Judas closed his eyes, and for a whole age neither breathed, nor saw, nor lived, but only listened.

But lo! with a grating sound iron struck against iron, and time after time dull, short blows, and then the sharp nail penetrating the soft wood, and separating its particles is distinctly heard.

One hand. It is not yet too late!

The other hand. It is not yet too late!

A foot, the other foot! Is all lost?

He irresolutely opens his eyes, and sees how the cross is raised, and rocks, and is set fast in the trench. He sees how the hands of Jesus are convulsed by the tension, how painfully His arms stretch, how the wounds grow wider, and how the exhausted abdomen disappears under the ribs. The arms stretch more and more, grow thinner and whiter, and become dislocated from the shoulders, and the wounds of the nails redden and lengthen gradually—lo! in a moment they will be torn away. No. It stopped. All stopped. Only the ribs move up and down with the short, deep breathing.

On the very crown of the hill the cross is raised, and on it is the crucified Jesus. The horror and the dreams of Judas are realized, he gets up from his knees on which for some reason he had knelt, and gazes coldly around.

Thus does a stern conqueror look, when he has already determined in his heart to give over everything to destruction and death, and for the last time throws a glance over a rich foreign city, still alive with sound, but already phantom-like under the cold hand of death. And suddenly, as clearly as his terrible victory, Iscariot saw its ominous precariousness. What if they should suddenly understand? It is not yet too late! Jesus still lives. There He looks with entreating, sorrowing eyes.

What can prevent the thin film which covers the eyes of mankind, so thin that it seems hardly to exist at all, what can prevent it from rending? What if they should understand? What if suddenly, in all their threatening mass of men, women and children, they should advance, silently without a cry, and wipe out the soldiery, plunging them up to their ears in their own blood, should tear from the ground the accursed cross, and by the hands of all who remain alive should lift up the liberated Jesus above the summit of the hill! Osanna! Osanna!

Osanna? No! Better that Judas should lie on the ground. Better that he should lie upon the ground, and gnashing his teeth like a dog, should watch and wait until all these should rise up.

But what has come to Time? Now it almost stands still, so that one would wish to push it with the hands, to kick it, beat it with a whip like a lazy ass; now it rushes madly down some mountain or other, and catches its breath, and stretches out its hand in vain to stop itself. There weeps the mother of Jesus. Let them weep. What avail now her tears? nay the tears of all the mothers in the world?

"What are tears?" asks Judas, and madly pushes unyielding Time, beats it with his fists, curses it like a slave. It belongs to some one else, and therefore is unamenable to discipline. Oh! if only it belonged to Judas! But it belongs to all these people who are weeping, laughing, chattering as in the market. It belongs to the sun; it belongs to the cross; to the heart of Jesus, which is dying so slowly.

What an abject heart has Judas! He lays his hand upon it, but it cries out: "Osanna," so loud that all may hear. He presses it to the ground, but it cries, "Osanna, Osanna!" like a babbler who scatters holy mysteries broadcast through the street.

"Be still! Be still!"

Suddenly a loud broken lamentation, dull cries, the last hurried movements towards the cross. What is it? Have they understood at last?

No, Jesus is dying. But can this be? Yes, Jesus is dying. His pale hands are motionless, but short convulsions run over His face, and breast, and legs. But can this be? Yes, He is dying. His breathing becomes less frequent. It ceases. No, there is yet one sigh, Jesus is still upon the earth. But is there another? No, no, no. Jesus is dead.

It is finished. Osanna! Osanna!

His horror and his dreams are realized. Who will now snatch the victory from the hands of Iscariot?

It is finished. Let all people on earth stream to Golgotha, and shout with their million throats, "Osanna! Osanna!" And let a sea of blood and tears be poured out at its foot, and they will find only the shameful cross and a dead Jesus!

Calmly and coldly Iscariot surveys the dead, letting his gaze rest for a moment on that neck, which he had kissed only yesterday with a farewell kiss; and slowly goes away. Now all Time belongs to him, and he walks without hurry; now all the World belongs to him, and he steps firmly, like a ruler, like a king, like one who is infinitely and joyfully alone in the world. He observes the mother of Jesus, and says to her sternly—

"Thou weepest, mother? Weep, weep, and long will all the mothers upon earth weep with thee: until I come with Jesus and destroy death."

What does he mean? Is he mad, or is he

mocking—this Traitor? He is serious, and his face is stern, and his eyes no longer dart about in mad haste. Lo! he stands still, and with cold attention views a new, diminished earth.

It is become small, and he feels the whole of it under his feet. He looks at the little mountains, quietly reddening under the last rays of the sun, and he feels the mountains under his feet.

He looks at the sky opening wide its azure mouth; he looks at the small round disc of the sun, which vainly strives to singe and dazzle, and he feels the sky and the sun under his feet. Infinitely and joyfully alone, he proudly feels the impotence of all forces which operate in the world, and has cast them all into the abyss.

He walks farther on, with quiet, masterful steps. And Time goes neither forward nor back: obediently it marches in step with him in all its invisible immensity.

It is finished.

IX

As an old cheat, coughing, smiling fawningly, bowing incessantly, Judas Iscariot the Traitor appeared before the Sanhedrin. It was the day after the murder of Jesus, about mid-day. There they were all, His judges and murderers: the aged Annas with his sons, exact and disgusting likenesses of their father, and his son-in-law Caiaphas, devoured by ambition, and all the other members of the Sanhedrin, whose names have been snatched from the memory of mankind—rich and distinguished Sadducees, proud in their power and knowledge of the Law.

In silence they received the Traitor, their haughty faces remaining motionless, as though no one had entered. And even the very least, and most insignificant among them, to whom the others paid no attention, lifted up his bird-like face and looked as though no one had entered.

Judas bowed and bowed and bowed, and they looked on in silence: as though it was not a human being that had entered, but only an unclean insect that had crept in, and which they had not observed. But Judas Iscariot was not the man to be perturbed: they kept silence, and he kept on bowing, and thought that if it was necessary to go on bowing till evening, he could do so.

At length Caiaphas inquired impatiently—

"What do you want?"

Judas bowed once more, and said in a loud voice—

"It is I, Judas Iscariot, who betrayed to you Jesus of Nazareth."

"Well, what of that? You have received your due. Go away!" ordered Annas; but Judas appeared unconscious of the command, and continued bowing. Glancing at him, Caiaphas asked Annas—

"How much did you give?"

"Thirty pieces of silver."

Caiaphas laughed, and even the grey-bearded Annas laughed, too, and over all their proud faces there crept a smile of enjoyment: and the one with the bird-like face even laughed. Judas, perceptibly blanching, hastily caught up with the words—

"That's right! Certainly it was very little; but is Judas discontented, does Judas call out that he has been robbed? He is satisfied. Has he not contributed to a holy cause— yes, a holy. Do not the most sage people now listen to Judas, and think: He is one of us, this Judas Iscariot; he is our brother, our friend, this Judas Iscariot, the Traitor! Does not Annas want to kneel down and kiss the hand of Judas? Only Judas will not allow it; he is a coward, he is afraid they will bite him."

Caiaphas said—

"Drive the dog out! What's he barking about?"

"Get along with you. We have no time

to listen to your babbling," said Annas imperturbably.

Judas drew himself up and closed his eyes. The hypocrisy, which he had carried so lightly all his life, suddenly became an insupportable burden, and with one movement of his eyelashes he cast it from him. And when again he looked at Annas his glance was simple, direct, and terrible in its naked truthfulness. Neither to this did they pay any attention.

"You want to be driven out with sticks!" cried Caiaphas.

Panting under the weight of the terrible words, which he was lifting higher and higher, in order to hurl them hence upon the heads of the judges, Judas hoarsely asked—

"But you know . . . you know . . . who He was . . . He, whom you yesterday condemned and crucified?"

"We know. Go away!"

With one word he would rend directly that thin film which was spread over their eyes, and all the earth would stagger beneath the weight of the merciless truth! They had a soul, they should be deprived of it; they had a life, they should lose their life; they had light before their eyes, eternal darkness and horror should cover them. Osanna! Osanna!

And these words, these terrible words, were tearing his throat asunder—

"He was no deceiver. He was innocent and pure. Do you hear? Judas deceived you. He betrayed to you an innocent man."

He waits. He hears the aged unconcerned voice of Annas, saying—

"And is that all you want to say?"

"You seem not to have understood me," says Judas with dignity, turning pale. "Judas deceived you. He was innocent. You have slain the innocent."

He of the bird-like face smiles; but Annas is indifferent, Annas yawns. And Caiaphas yawns, too, and says wearily—

"What did they mean by talking to me about the intellect of Judas Iscariot? He is simply a fool, and a tedious one, too."

"What?" cried Judas, all suffused with dark madness. "But who are you, the clever ones! Judas deceived you—hear! It was not Him that he betrayed—but you—you wiseacres, you, the powerful, you he betrayed to a shameful death, which will not end, throughout the ages. Thirty pieces of silver! Well, well. But that is the price of *your* blood—blood filthy as the dish-water which the women throw out of the gates of their houses. Oh! Annas, old, grey, stupid Annas, chokeful of the Law, why did you not give one silver piece, just one *obolus* more? At this price you will go down through the ages!"

"Be off!" cried Caiaphas, growing purple in the face. But Annas stopped him with a motion of the hand, and asked Judas as unconcernedly as ever—

"Is that all?"

"Verily, if I were to go into the desert, and cry to the wild beasts: 'Wild beasts, have ye heard the price at which men valued their Jesus?'—what would the wild beasts do? They would creep out of the lairs, they would howl with anger, they would forget their fear of mankind, and would all come here to devour you! If I were to say to the sea: 'Sea, knowest thou the price at which men valued their Jesus?' If I were to say to the mountains: 'Mountains, know ye the price at which men valued their Jesus?' Then the sea and the mountains would leave their places, assigned to them from ages, and would come here and fall upon your heads!"

"Does Judas wish to become a prophet? He speaks so loud!" mockingly remarked he of the bird-like face, with an ingratiating glance at Caiaphas.

"To-day I saw a pale sun. It was looking at the earth, and saying: 'Where is the Man?' To-day I saw a scorpion. It was sitting upon a stone and laughing said: 'Where is the Man?' I went near and looked into its eyes. And it laughed and said: 'Where is the Man? I do not see Him!' Where is the Man? I ask you, I do not see Him—or is Judas become blind, poor Judas Iscariot!"

And Iscariot began to weep aloud.

He was, during those minutes, like one out of his mind, and Caiaphas turned away, making a contemptuous gesture with his hand. But Annas considered a little, and then said—

"I perceive, Judas, that you really have received but little, and that disturbs you. Here is some more money, take it and give it to your children."

He threw something, which rang shrilly. The sound had not died away, before another, like it, strangely prolonged the clinking.

Judas had hastily flung the pieces of silver and the *oboles* into the faces of the high priest and of the judges, returning the price paid for Jesus. The pieces of money flew in a curved shower, falling on their faces, and on the table, and rolling about the floor.

Some of the judges closed their hands with the palms outwards; others leapt from their places, and shouted and scolded. Judas, trying to hit Annas, threw the last coin, after which his trembling hand had been long fumbling in his wallet, spat in anger, and went out.

"Well, well," he mumbled, as he passed swiftly through the streets, scaring the children. "It seems that thou didst weep, Judas? Was Caiaphas really right when he said that Judas Iscariot was a fool? He who weeps in the day of his great revenge is not worthy of it—know'st thou that, Judas? Let not thine eyes deceive thee; let not thine heart lie to thee; flood not the fire with tears, Judas Iscariot!"

The disciples were sitting in mournful silence, listening to what was going on without. There was still danger that the vengeance of Jesus' enemies might not confine itself to Him, and so they were all expecting a visit from the guard, and perhaps more executions. Near to John, to whom, as the beloved disciple, the death of Jesus was especially grievous, sat Mary Magdalene, and Matthew trying to comfort him in an undertone. Mary, whose face was swollen with weeping, softly stroked his luxurious curling hair with her hand, while Matthew said didactically, in the words of Solomon—

"The long suffering is better than a hero: and he that ruleth his own spirit than one who taketh a city."

At this moment Judas knocked loudly at the door, and came in. All started up in terror, and at first were not sure who it was; but when they recognized the hated countenance, the red-haired, bulbous head, they uttered a simultaneous cry.

Peter raised both hands and shouted—

"Get out of this, Traitor. Get out, or I will kill you."

But the others looked more carefully at the face and eyes of the Traitor, and said nothing, merely whispering in terror—

"Leave him alone, leave him alone! He is possessed with a devil."

Judas waited until they had quite done, and then cried out in a loud voice—

"Hail, ye eyes of Judas Iscariot! Ye have

just seen the cold-blooded murderers. Lo! Where is Jesus? I ask you, where is Jesus?"

There was something compelling in the hoarse voice of Judas, and Thomas replied obediently—

"You know yourself, Judas, that our Master was crucified yesterday."

"But how came you to permit it? Where was your love? Thou, Beloved Disciple, and thou, Rock, where were you all when they were crucifying your Friend on the tree?"

"What could we do, judge thou," said Thomas, with a gesture of protest.

"Thou askest that, Thomas? Very well!" and Judas threw his head back, and fell upon him angrily. "He who loves does not ask what can be done—he goes and does it—he weeps, he bites, he throttles the enemy, and breaks his bones! He, that is, who loves! If your son were drowning would you go into the city and inquire of the passers by: 'What must I do? My son is drowning!' No, you would rather throw yourself into the water and drown with him. One who loved would!"

Peter replied grimly to the violent speech of Judas—

"I drew a sword, but He Himself forbade."

"Forbade? And you obeyed!" jeered Judas. "Peter, Peter, how could you listen to Him? Does He know anything of men, and of fighting?"

"He who does not submit to Him goes to hell fire."

"Then why did you not go, Peter? Hell fire! What's that? Now, supposing you had gone—what good's your soul to you, if you dare not throw it into the fire, if you want to?"

"Silence!" cried John, rising. "He Himself willed this sacrifice. His sacrifice is beautiful!"

"Is a sacrifice ever beautiful, Beloved Disciple? Wherever there is a sacrifice, then there is an executioner, and there traitors!

Sacrifice—that is suffering for one and disgrace for all the others! Traitors, traitors, what have ye done with the world? Now they look at it from above and below, and laugh and cry: 'Look at that world, upon it they crucified Jesus!' And they spit on it—as I do!"

Judas angrily spat on the ground.

"He took upon Him the sin of all mankind. His sacrifice is beautiful," John insisted.

"No! you have taken all sin upon yourselves. You, Beloved Disciple, will not a race of traitors take their beginning from you, a pusillanimous and lying breed? O blind men, what have ye done with the earth? You have done your best to destroy it, ye will soon be kissing the cross on which ye crucified Jesus! Yes, yes, Judas gives ye his word that ye will kiss the cross!"

"Judas, don't revile!" roared Peter, pushing. "How could we slay all His enemies? They are so many!"

"And thou, Peter!" exclaimed John in anger, "dost thou not perceive that he is possessed of Satan. Leave us, Tempter! Thou'rt full of lies. The Teacher forbade us to kill."

"But did He forbid you to die? Why are you alive, when He is dead? Why do your feet walk, why does your tongue talk trash, why do your eyes blink, when He is dead, motionless, speechless? How do your cheeks dare to be red, John, when His are pale? How can you dare to shout, Peter, when He is silent? What do? ye ask Judas? And Judas answers you, the magnificent, bold Judas Iscariot replies: Die! You ought to have fallen on the road, to have seized the soldiers by the sword, by the hands, and drowned them in a sea of your own blood—yes, die, die! Better had it been, that His Father should have cause to cry out with horror, when you all enter there!"

Judas ceased with raised head. Suddenly he noticed the remains of a meal upon the table. With strange surprise, curiously, as though for the first time in his life he looked on food, he examined it, and slowly asked—

"What is this? You have been eating? Perhaps you have also been sleeping?"

Peter, who had begun to feel Judas to be some one, who could command obedience, drooping his head, tersely replied: "I slept, I slept and ate!"

Thomas said, resolutely and firmly—

"This is all untrue, Judas. Just consider: if we had all died, who would have told the story of Jesus? Who would have conveyed His teaching to mankind if we had all died, Peter and John and I?"

"But what is the truth itself in the mouths of traitors? Does it not become a lie? Thomas, Thomas, dost thou not understand, that thou art now only a sentinel at the grave of dead Truth. The sentinel falls asleep, and the thief cometh and carries away the truth; say, where is the truth? Cursed be thou, Thomas! Fruitless, and a beggar shalt thou be throughout the ages, and all you with him, accursed ones!"

"Accursed be thou thyself, Satan!" cried John, and James and Matthew and all the other disciples repeated his cry; only Peter held his peace.

"I am going to Him," said Judas, stretching his powerful hand on high. "Who will follow Iscariot to Jesus?"

"I—I also go with thee," cried Peter, rising.

But John and the others stopped him in horror, saying—

"Madman! Thou hast forgotten, that he betrayed the Master into the hands of His enemies."

Peter began to lament bitterly, striking his breast with his fist—

"Whither, then, shall I go? O Lord! whither shall I go?"

* * * * *

Judas had long ago, during his solitary walks, marked the place where he intended to make an end of himself after the death of Jesus.

It was upon a hill high above Jerusalem. There stood there only one tree, bent and twisted by the wind, which had torn it on all sides, half withered. One of its broken, crooked branches stretched out towards Jerusalem, as though in blessing or in threat, and this one Judas had chosen on which to hang a noose.

But the walk to the tree was long and tedious, and Judas Iscariot was very weary. The small, sharp stones, scattered under his feet, seemed continually to drag him backwards, and the hill was high, stern, and malign, exposed to the wind. Judas was obliged to sit down several times to rest, and panted heavily, while behind him, through the clefts of the rock, the mountain breathed cold upon his back.

"Thou too art against me, accursed one!" said Judas contemptuously, as he breathed with difficulty, and swayed his heavy head, in which all the thoughts were now petrifying.

Then he raised it suddenly, and opening wide his now fixed eyes, angrily muttered—

"No, they were too bad for Judas. Thou hearest Jesus? Wilt Thou trust me now? I am coming to Thee. Meet me kindly, I am weary—very weary. Then Thou and I, embracing like brothers, will return to earth. Will we not?"

Again he swayed his petrifying head, and again he opened his eyes, mumbling—

"But maybe Thou wilt be angry with Judas when he arrives? And Thou wilt not trust him? And wilt send me to hell? Well! what then? I will go to hell. And in Thy hell fire I will weld iron, and weld iron, and demolish Thy heaven. Dost approve? Then Thou wilt believe in me. Then Thou wilt come back with me to earth, wilt Thou not, Jesus?"

Eventually Judas reached the top and the crooked tree, and there the wind began to torment him. And when Judas rebuked it, it began to blow soft and low, and took leave and flew away.

"Right! But as for them, they are curs!" said Judas, making a slip-knot. And since the rope might fail him and break, he hung it over a precipice, so that if it broke, he would meet his death upon the stones all the same. And before he shoved himself off the brink with his foot, and hanged himself, Judas Iscariot once more anxiously prepared Jesus for his coming—

"Yes, meet me kindly, Jesus, I am very weary."

He leapt. The rope strained, but held. His neck stretched, but his hands and feet were crossed, and hung down as though damp.

He died. Thus, in the course of two days, one after another, Jesus of Nazareth and Judas Iscariot, the Traitor, left the world.

All the night through, like some monstrous fruit, Judas swayed over Jerusalem, and the wind kept turning his face now to the city, and now to the desert—as though it wished to exhibit Judas to both city and desert. But in whichever direction his face, distorted by death, was turned, his red eyes suffused with blood, and now as like one another as two brothers, incessantly looked towards the sky. In the morning some sharp-sighted person perceived Judas hanging above the city, and cried out in horror.

People came and took him down, and knowing who he was, threw him into a deep ravine, into which they were in the habit of throwing dead horses and cats and other carrion.

This same evening all the believers knew of the terrible death of the Traitor, and the next day it was known to all Jerusalem. Stony Judæa knew of it and green Galilee; and from one sea to the other, distant as it was, the news flew of the death of the Traitor.

Neither faster nor slower, but with equal pace with time itself, it went, and as there is no end to time so will there be no end to the stories about the Traitor Judas and his terrible death.

And all—both good and bad—will equally anathematize his shameful memory; and among all peoples, past and present, will he remain alone in his cruel destiny—Judas Iscariot, the Traitor.

BEN TOBIT

On that terrible day when the world's act of injustice was consummated, and Jesus Christ was crucified at Golgotha between two thieves, on that day from the earliest morning Ben Tobit, a merchant of Jerusalem, had been suffering from an unendurable toothache.

It had begun the evening before, when it attacked slightly the right jaw. The tooth, the last before the wisdom-tooth, felt as though it protruded a little beyond the others, and when he touched it with his tongue it produced a slight feeling of pain. However, after eating the pain left him entirely, and Ben Tobit forgot all about it, and became quite at his ease. He had only that day made a profitable exchange of his old ass for a strong young one, and so he was in a remarkably good humour, and paid no attention to the ominous symptoms. He slept well and soundly; but just before dawn something began to arouse him, as though some one was calling him to go about some important business, and when Ben Tobit woke in a rage his teeth were aching, aching openly and viciously, with all the plenitude of a sharp wimbling pain. It was no longer possible to decide whether it was only yesterday's tooth, or whether the others were joining in the aching. His whole mouth and head were filled with a terrible feeling of pain, as though he had been compelled to chew a thousand sharp red-hot nails. He put some water into his mouth from the earthen ewer, and for a time the fierceness of the pain went away. His teeth twinged, indeed, and seemed to surge like waves; but even this feeling was pleasant compared with the former. Ben Tobit lay down again, called to mind his new donkey, and thought how fortunate he would have been but for his teeth, and was at the point of falling to sleep. But the water had got warm, and in the course of five minutes the pain returned worse than ever, and Ben

Tobit sat up in his bed, and rocked himself like a pendulum. His whole face became wrinkled, and gathered up to his big nose, on which, paled as it was with suffering, had settled a drop of cold sweat. Thus rocking himself, and groaning with pain, he met the first rays of that sun, which was doomed to see Golgotha with its three crosses, and to grow dark with horror and grief.

Ben Tobit was a good and kind man who hated injustice, still, when his wife awoke, scarcely opening his mouth he rated her very unpleasantly, and complained that he had been left alone like a jackal to howl and huddle in agony. His wife bore patiently with his undeserved reproaches, since she knew that they did not proceed from badness of heart; and she brought many excellent nostrums: clarified rats' dung, to be laid upon the cheek, a sharp extract of scorpion, and a genuine fragment of the Tablets of the Law, which were broken by Moses. After the application of the rat's dung he became a little better; but not for long. And so, too, after the extract and the piece of stone; but each time after a brief respite the pain returned with renewed force. During the short minutes of rest Ben Tobit consoled himself with thinking about his donkey, and built castles in the air about it; but when he became worse again he groaned, and was angry with his wife, and threatened to dash his head against a stone if the pain did not cease. And all the time he kept walking from corner to corner on the flat roof of his house, ashamed to go near to the outer edge of it, because his head was all bound up in a handkerchief like a woman's. Several times children ran close to him and talked in hurried voices something about "Jesus of Nazareth." Ben Tobit stopped and listened to them for a little, screwing up his face, but soon he would angrily stamp his feet, and make them go. He was a kind man and loved children, but just then he was angry that they should worry him with such trifles. It was also annoying that in the streets and on the neighbouring roofs much people were gathered together, who had nothing to do but to look with curiosity at Ben Tobit, who was muffled in a handkerchief like a woman. He was just on the point of going down-stairs, when his wife said to him—

"Look; they are leading the robbers to execution, perhaps that will distract you."

"Do let me alone, please. Don't you see how I am suffering?" angrily replied Ben Tobit.

But in his wife's words there sounded a vague promise, that his toothache might leave him, and so he unwillingly drew near to the parapet. Inclining his head on one side, shutting one eye, and leaning his cheek on his hand, he made a fastidiously sorrowful face, and looked down below.

In the narrow street which led up to the hill an immense crowd was surging, enveloped in dust and incessant cries. In the midst of it, bending under the weight of the crosses, moved the criminals, and over them the whips of the Roman soldiers twisted like black serpents. One, He with the long light locks in a torn blood-stained shirt, stumbled against a stone in His path and fell. The shouts became louder, and the crowd, like a many-coloured wave of the sea, closed over the prostrate one. Ben Tobit was suddenly convulsed with a twinge of pain. It felt as if some one had thrust a red-hot needle into his tooth and given it a twist there. He groaned, "Oh! oh! oh!" and left the parapet, fastidiously indifferent, and angry.

"How they shout!" he said in envy, picturing to himself their wide-open mouths with strong, sound teeth, and how he would have shouted too if only he had been well. And that picture caused his tooth to pain him more fiercely, and he kept shaking his enveloped head and bellowing—

"Moo! moo!"

"They talked of His having healed the blind," said his wife. She had not left the parapet, and threw a small stone down to the place where Jesus, who had been got on to His feet by blows of the whip, was now moving slowly on.

"Oh, indeed! Then He might as well cure my toothache," Ben Tobit replied in irony, and irritably added, with bitterness, "What a dust they do make! Just like a herd of cattle! They ought to be dispersed with a stick! Help me down, Sarah."

His wife turned out to be right. The spectacle had somewhat distracted Ben Tobit, and possibly the rat's dung had done some good in the end; at all events, he managed to get to sleep. When he woke the pain was almost gone, only his right jaw was a little bit swollen, so little as to be scarcely noticeable. Indeed, his wife said that it was quite imperceptible; but Ben Tobit smiled slyly, as knowing how kind his wife was, and how she liked to say what was agreeable. A neighbour, Samuel the tanner, arrived, and Ben Tobit took him to see his new donkey, and listened proudly to the glowing encomiums of himself and his beast.

Afterwards, at the request of the curious Sarah, they all three went to Golgotha to look at those who had been crucified. On the way

Ben Tobit kept recounting to Samuel from the very beginning how yesterday he had felt a twinge in his right jaw, and how he had woke afterwards in the night with a terrible pain. By way of illustration, he made a face of suffering, shut his eyes, nodded his head and groaned, and the grey-bearded Samuel wagged his head in compassion, and said—

"Dear, dear! how painful!"

Ben Tobit was pleased with the appreciation, and went through the whole story again; and then referred to the long-distant time, when he had lost his first tooth, one of the lower ones on the left side. Thus engaged in lively conversation they arrived at Golgotha. The sun, which had been doomed to illumine the world on that dreadful day, was already sinking behind the distant hills, and a narrow bright red stripe, like a track of blood, glowed in the west. Against this, as a background, the dark crosses were faintly distinguishable, and at the foot of the centre cross some kneeling figures formed a vague patch of white.

The crowd had long ago dispersed. It became cold, and Ben Tobit, with a casual glance at the figures on the crosses, took Samuel by the hand and gently turned him in the direction of his home. He felt especially voluble, and he wanted to tell all about his toothache. Thus they walked, and Ben Tobit, at Samuel's sympathetic head-shakes and exclamations, made a face of suffering, shook his head, and groaned artistically. And out of the deep clefts and from the distant parched plains rose the dark night. It was as though it wished to hide from the sight of heaven—earth's great crime.

ELEAZAR

I

WHEN Eleazar left the grave, where he had spent three days and three nights in the mysterious power of death, and returned alive to his house, for a long time those ominous peculiarities in him, which afterwards caused his very name to be dreaded by his contemporaries, passed unnoticed.

Rejoicing gaily in his return to life, Eleazer's friends and relatives continually caressed him, and satisfied their eager regard for him by anxiety about his food, and drink, and new clothes. They dressed him sumptuously in the bright coloured clothes of hope and laughter, and when, like a bridegroom in wedding garments, he was seated once more at table in their midst eating and drinking, they wept in deep emotion, and called in the neighbours to look at him, who had so miraculously risen from the dead. There came neighbours, and rejoiced in deep emotion; there came strangers from distant towns and villages, and in boisterous exclamations expressed their profound respect for the miracle—like bees they buzzed about the house of Mary and Martha.

And that which appeared new in the face and in the movements of Eleazar they explained naturally, as traces of the serious illness, and of the violent shocks he had gone through.

On Eleazar's temples, under his eyes, in the hollows of his cheeks there lay a thick earthy blueness; clay-blue were also his long fingers, which near the nails, that had grown in the grave, had turned more livid and dark. Here and there on the lips, and on the body his skin, swollen in the grave, had burst; and in those places there remained thin reddish cracks, shining as though covered with transparent mica. He had become obese. His body, swollen in the grave, retained those monstrous dimensions, those frightful protuberances, beneath which one felt the fetid moisture of decomposition. But the heavy smell of the corpse, which permeated Eleazar's burial clothes and, as it seemed, his very body, soon faded away, and in the course of time the blueness of his hands and face faded somewhat, and the reddish cracks of the skin became smooth, although they never disappeared altogether. With such a face came Eleazar before people in his second life, and it seemed quite natural to those who had seen him buried.

Thus, with the face of a corpse, over which death had reigned in darkness for three days, in sumptuous wedding garments, grave and silent, fearfully changed and peculiar (though that was not yet acknowledged by any one), he sat at the feast amongst his friends and relatives. The musicians played. It was as though bees were buzzing, and crickets chirruping, and birds singing over the happy house of Mary and Martha.

II

Some one heedlessly raised the veil. Some one carelessly, by the mere breath of an idle word, broke the bright charm, and revealed the truth in its ugly nakedness. The thought had scarce become clear in his mind, when his lips smilingly asked—

"Why dost thou not tell us, Eleazar, what it was like there?"

All were silent, struck by the question, as if they had only just suspected that Eleazar had been dead for three days; and they stared curiously at him, waiting for a reply. But Eleazar kept silence.

"Thou dost not wish to tell us?" asked the questioner in wonderment. "Was it so dreadful there?"

And again his words outran his thoughts; for had he thought before he spoke he would not have asked the question, which at that very moment made his own heart contract with unendurable terror. All became uneasy, and with anguish they waited for Eleazar's words, but he kept silence, cold and grave, with his eyes cast down. The musicians went on playing, but presently the silence influenced them too, and as water extinguishes scattered embers so the silence suppressed the gay sounds, and all was still.

That had taken place the third day after Eleazar had come forth from the grave. Since then many people had experienced the baleful power of his look, but neither those who had been subdued by it for ever, nor those who had found in the very primary sources of life, mysterious as death itself, the will to resist, could ever explain the horrible thing that lay immovable in the depth of the black pupils of his eyes. The sun did not cease shining when he looked, the fountains did not cease to splash, the sky overhead remained just as cloudless and blue as ever, but the man who fell under his mysterious gaze felt no more the warmth of the sun, heard no more the sound of the fountain, and recognized not the sky of his native land. Sometimes such an one would weep bitterly; sometimes he desperately tore his hair and called madly to others for help. But more often it would happen that the man began to die, indifferently and calmly. He was many long years a-dying before the eyes of all, and he died pale, languid and weary, like a tree that quietly withers away on a stony soil. And the former, those who cried out and raved, sometimes came back to life; but the latter—never.

III

None took any care of Eleazar, no friend remained to him, and the great desert that surrounded the Holy City crept up to the very threshold of his dwelling. One after the other his sisters, Mary and Martha, had left him. For a long time Martha wished not to forsake him, for she knew not who would feed and compassionate him; so she wept and prayed. But one night, when the wind swept over the desert, and with a whistling sound the cypresses bent over the roof, she quietly dressed herself and silently departed.

As though he had been a leper he was shunned by all, and they would have put a bell round his neck so as to avoid him on meeting, had not some one, turning pale, said that it would be very terrifying if in the night Eleazar's bell were to be heard under the windows; and all, turning pale, agreed with him.

And as he did not take care of himself, he might have died of starvation, had not the neighbours, from an indefinable fear, left him something to eat. This was brought to him by children. Left to the mercy of time and the desert, his house was gradually falling into ruins, and his hungry, bleating goats had long ago dispersed among his neighbours. His wedding garments had gone to decay. As he had donned them on that happy day when the musicians played, so he had worn them all the time without any change, as though he saw no difference between old and new, between torn clothes and good ones. Their bright colours had gradually tarnished and faded away; the snarling dogs of the town and the sharp thorns of the desert had turned their dainty texture into rags.

During the daytime, when the merciless sun was the death of every living thing, and even the scorpions were driven in beneath the stones, and shrivelled there from a mad desire to sting, he would sit motionless under the rays of the sun with his livid face and shaggy wild beard tilted upwards.

And when its flattened, red-gold sphere sank to the level of the ground, Eleazar would go away into the desert, and walk straight towards the sun, as though wishing to overtake it. He always walked straight towards the sun, and those who tried to follow him, and to find out what he was doing in the desert by night, had indelibly engraved on their memory the black silhouette of a tall, stout man on the red ground of a huge compressed disc. They were driven away by the night with all its terrors, and so they failed to find out what Eleazar was doing in the desert; but the image of the black on the red ground was branded on their brain, and did not pass away.

But there were people who lived far away

who had never seen Eleazar, but had only heard of him. With an impertinent curiosity, which is stronger than fear, and indeed feeds on it, with raillery concealed in their hearts, they came to him, who sat in the sun, and entered into conversation with him. There came brave warriors, that knew no fear, clanking their arms; there came happy youths with songs and laughter, and there ran in for a minute preoccupied business men jingling their money, and haughty priests of the temple left their staves at Eleazar's door; but no one departed the same man that he came. One and the same terrible shadow came over their souls, and gave a new aspect to the old familiar world.

IV

At that time there lived in Rome a famous sculptor. Out of clay, marble, and bronze he created forms of gods and men, and such was their divine beauty, that people called it immortal. But he himself was discontented, and used to say that there was something more, the truly most beautiful, which he was unable to express in marble or bronze.

"I have not gathered yet the radiance of the moon; I have not grasped yet the rays of the sun; and there is no soul in my marble, no life in my beautiful bronze," he would say.

When vague rumours of Eleazar had reached him, he consulted his wife and friends, and set out on the long journey to Judæa, in order to see him, who had miraculously risen from the dead. The stories he had heard of Eleazar did not frighten him. He had meditated much upon death, and he misliked it; but neither did he like those who confused it with life. He even had a certain ambitious desire to convince Eleazar of the truth of his own views, and to bring back his soul to life even as his body had been brought back. This seemed to him all the easier, because the rumours of him, though fearful and strange, did not reveal the whole truth about him, but only gave vague warning of something dreadful.

Eleazar had just risen from a stone to follow the setting sun into the desert, when a rich Roman, accompanied by an armed slave, approached him, and sonorously called him by name—

"Eleazar!"

Eleazar perceived a proud figure with a handsome countenance, clothed in bright garments studded with precious stones which sparkled in the sun. The reddish rays of the setting sun imparted to his head and his face the colour of dimly shining bronze, and Eleazar observed this fact.

Resignedly he reseated himself, and wearily cast down his eyes.

"No, thou art not good looking, my poor Eleazar," said the Roman calmly, playing with his gold chain. "Thou art even frightful, my poor friend. Wilt thou let me stay over night with thee? It is already late, and I have no shelter."

No one had ever yet asked to spend the night at Eleazar's house.

"I have no bed," he answered.

"Oh, I am somewhat of a campaigner, and can sleep sitting," said the Roman. "Let us light the fire. . . ."

"I have no fire."

"Then we shall have a chat in the dark like two friends. I suppose thou hast some wine. . . ."

"I have no wine."

The Roman laughed.

"Oh, now I understand why thou art so gloomy, and carest not for thy second life. No wine! Well, then we'll do without it; are there not words which intoxicate no less than Falernian?"

With a wave of his hand he dismissed his slave; and they two were left together. Again the sculptor began to speak; but with the departing sun life seemed, as it were, to be fading out of his speech, and his words grew colourless and empty; it was as though they were stumbling on unsteady feet, as though they were tottering and falling, soaked with the wine of anguish and despair. Black gaps appeared between them, as distant suggestions of a great void, and a great darkness beyond.

The sun had already disappeared, a giant black shadow had begun to run from the east, as though enormous bare feet were scuffling over the sand, and the draught caused by the rapid running sent a shiver down the spine.

Night had come on, and the air was filled with heavy blackness.

"I shall be glad when the sun rises again to-morrow. . . . Dost thou not know that I am a great sculptor?—at least I am so called by my friends. I 'create'—yes, that is the word for it—but it requires the daylight. To the cold marble I give life, I melt in the fire the sounding bronze, in the bright, hot fire. . . . Why didst thou touch me with thy hand?"

"Let us go," said Eleazar; "thou art my guest."

They went into the house, and the long night came upon the earth.

The slave waited in vain for his master, and came to them when the sun was already high. He saw Eleazar and his master sitting side by side right under its burning rays, looking up and silent.

The slave began to weep, and cried out aloud—

"My lord, what is the matter with thee? My lord!"

That same day they set out for Rome. The sculptor's household took alarm at the frightful change that had come over him; but he appeased them, saying meaningly—

"I have found it."

In the same muddy clothes, which he had not changed during the whole of the journey, he set to work, and the marble began submissively to ring under the resounding strokes of his hammer. Long and eagerly he worked, admitting no one. At last, one morning, he announced that his work was completed, and sent to invite his friends, the stern appraisers and connoisseurs of art.

His friends cast a glance on his work, and a shadow of profound sorrow passed over their faces. It was something monstrous, something that had none of the forms familiar to the eye, but not devoid of a hint at some new, unknown image. And under one of the strangely accentuated protuberances they discovered by chance an exquisitely chiselled butterfly with diaphanous winglets, which seemed to throb with an impotent desire to fly.

"Why this wonderful butterfly, Aurelius?" some one asked, with a certain hesitation.

"I know not," answered the sculptor.

But it was necessary to tell him the truth, and so one of his friends, the one who loved him best said firmly—

"This is ugly, my poor friend. It must be destroyed. Give me a hammer."

And with two strokes he destroyed the monstrous mass, leaving only the exquisitely chiselled butterfly.

Since then Aurelius has created nothing. Only when his friends talked to him too much and too long about "the beautiful," he would reply, wearily and languidly—

"But surely all that is false. . . ."

And in the daytime, when the sun was shining, he would go into his luxurious, artistic garden, and selecting a spot where there was no shadow, he would expose his bare head and dim eyes to the glare and heat of the sun. Red and white butterflies would flutter about, while the splashing water which flowed from the distorted mouth of a blissfully drunken Satyr dropped into the marble basin; but he would sit motionless, like a faint reflection of the one that sat in the far, far distance just as motionless under the fiery sun at the very gate of the stony desert.

V

And behold, the great divine Augustus himself sent for Eleazar.

They clothed him sumptuously in festal wedding garments. But the roads he had to travel were deserted: all his native country cursed the hateful name of him who had miraculously risen from the dead, and the people dispersed at the first rumour of his dreaded approach.

Then they took him by sea. It was the best appointed, but at the same time the most mournful, ship that ever was reflected by the azure waves of the Mediterranean Sea. There were many people on board her, but she was as silent and still as the tomb. The water seemed to cry in despair, as it passed on either side of her bold, beautiful curving stem. Eleazar sat there lonely, exposing his bare head to the sun, listened to the swirl of the water rushing by, and kept silence. At a distance—a confused crowd of melancholy shadows—lay or sat the seamen and the envoys, languid and without energy. If at this moment a thunderstorm had struck the ship, and the winds had rent her red sails, she would probably have perished, since none of those upon her had either the strength or the desire to struggle for bare life.

Indifferently Eleazar entered the streets of the eternal city. There were chariots hurrying by, there were crowds of strong, handsome, haughty men, the builders of the eternal city, and the proud participants of its life. Songs resounded in the air; fountains and women laughed with pearly laughter; topers moralized, and the sober listened to them with a smile; horseshoes rattled on the paving-stones. . . . "Who dares to be dismal in Rome?" said the citizens in indignation, and frowned. But two days later the whole of gossiping Rome was aware of the arrival of him who had miraculously risen from the dead, and all shunned him in dread.

But there were many daring people as well who wished to test their strength, and in answer to their senseless call Eleazar would obediently visit them. Preoccupied with the affairs of State, the Emperor delayed his interview with him, and for a whole week Eleazar went about among the people.

Behold, he came to a merry drunkard, and the toper met him with a smile on his red lips.

"Drink, Eleazar, drink!" shouted he. "Oh, how will Augustus laugh when he sees thee drunk!"

Women disguised in roses and wine

laughed also, and the petals from their wreaths of roses fell on Eleazar's livid hands. But once the drunkard looked into his eyes, his mirth was ended for ever. He remained drunk for all his life. He did not drink, but he remained drunk all the same; and instead of cheerful reveries, such as are inspired by wine, horrible dreams overshadowed his wretched head.

Behold, Eleazar came to a youth and a maiden who loved one another, and were beautiful in their love. Proudly and firmly encircling his sweetheart's waist with his arm, the youth said, with quiet sympathy—

"Look at us, Eleazar, and rejoice with us. Is there anything stronger than love?"

And Eleazar looked. And they continued to love each other all their lives, but their love became dismal and gloomy. Thrown by the incomprehensible life-force into each other's arms, they mixed their kisses with tears, delectation with pain, and doubly felt themselves slaves: obedient slaves of exacting life and submissive servants of the terribly silent Nothingness. Ever being united, and ever being disunited, they flashed like sparks, and like sparks they went out in the boundless darkness.

Behold, Eleazar visited a haughty sage, and the sage said to him—

"I know already all that thou canst tell me of the terrible, Eleazar. What else hast thou to terrify me with?"

But before long the sage felt that knowledge of the terrible is not the terrible, and that the sight of death is not death. And he felt that wisdom and folly are identically equal before the face of the infinite; for the infinite knows them not. And the borderline between knowledge and ignorance disappeared, the line between truth and falsehood, between top and bottom; and his amorphous thought became suspended in the void. Then he grasped his grey head with his hands, and cried out in desperation—

"I cannot think! I cannot think!"

Thus under the indifferent glance of him who had miraculously risen from the dead there perished everything that serves for the affirmation of life, for its meaning and its joys. People began to say that it would be dangerous to admit him to the Emperor, that it would be better to kill him, and to bury him secretly; and to give out that he had disappeared no one knew whither. Already swords were being sharpened, and youths devoted to the public good were self-denyingly preparing themselves for the task of the assassin, when Augustus commanded that Eleazar should come before him next morning, and thereby frustrated their cruel designs.

If they could not absolutely get rid of Eleazar, still they might somewhat soften the painful impression conveyed by the sight of his face. For this purpose they assembled skilful painters, enamellers and artists, and all night they worked at Eleazar's head. They cut his beard, curled it and gave it a neat and handsome appearance. The death-like lividness of his hands and face was unpleasant, so they removed it with the aid of pigments: they blanched his hands and rouged his cheeks.

The wrinkles of pain that furrowed his aged face were disgusting, so they filled them in, and painted them over, and smoothed them out, and on this fair surface they drew skilfully with fine brushes the wrinkles of good-natured laughter and of pleasant, kindly merriment.

Unconcernedly Eleazar submitted to everything they did to him, and was soon transformed into a naturally stout, good-looking old man, into the semblance of an even-tempered and good-natured grandfather of numerous grandchildren. But they did not venture to take off his wedding garments; and his eyes they could not change—those dark and terrible windows through which there looked out upon humanity the incomprehensible Beyond.

VI

Already Cæsar had learned who Eleazar was, and was prepared for the meeting. He was manly, was conscious of his enormous, invincible strength, and in his fateful duel with him who had risen from the dead he had no wish to rely upon weak human help. Man to man, face to face, he met Eleazar.

"Lift not thy glance to me, Eleazar," he commanded him as he entered the room. "I have heard that thy head is like that of Medusa, and transforms into stone every one on whom thou lookest. But I would contemplate thee, and converse with thee, before I am turned into stone," added he, with an august jocularity not devoid of awe.

Approaching Eleazar closely, he carefully examined his face and his strange festal robes. He was deceived by the skilful travesty, although his sight was sharp and piercing.

"Well! In appearance thou art not terrible, thou venerable old man. But all the worse for men, when the terrible assumes such a venerable and pleasant guise. Now let us converse. Well, then, who art thou?"

With some difficulty Eleazar replied—

"I was dead."

"I have heard about that. But who art thou now?"

Eleazar lingered in his reply, and at last repeated indifferently and dully—

"I was dead."

"Listen to me, thou unknown," said the Emperor; "my kingdom is the kingdom of the living, my people are the people of the living, and not of the dead. Thou art not wanted here. I know not who thou art, I know not what thou had seen there. But if thou liest, I hate thy lie; and if thou tellest the truth, I hate thy truth. In my breast I feel the throb of life, in my arms I feel might, and my proud thoughts like eagles fly through space. There, behind my back, under my protection, under the shadow of laws created by myself, there live, toil and rejoice human beings. Dost thou hear that wondrous harmony of life? Dost thou hear that war-cry that men hurl in the face of the future, challenging it to battle?"

Augustus stretched forth his arms prayerfully, and solemnly exclaimed, "Blessed be the great divine Life!"

But Eleazar kept silence, and with increased sternness the Emperor continued—

"Thou art superfluous here. Thou art a piteous remnant, not quite devoured as yet by death, and thou instillest into men sadness and distaste of life; like a canker-worm in the field thou eatest up the rich ears of joy, and sloughest off the slime of despair and sorrow. Thy truth is like a rusty sword in the hands of a night assassin; and as an assassin I shall hand thee over for execution. But first I wish to look at thine eyes. Mayhap it is only cowards who fear them; but in the brave they awake a thirst for struggle and victory, in which case thou deservest not execution, but reward. Look at me, Eleazar."

In the first moment it seemed to the divine Augustus that a friend looked at him—so soft, so attractive, so tenderly charming was Eleazar's glance. It promised not terror, but quiet rest; and as a tender sweetheart, a compassionate sister, or a doting mother appeared the Infinite. But stronger and stronger grew his tender embraces, and already a mouth thirsty for kisses was intercepting his breath. Through the tender tissue of his body there penetrated the iron of bones clamped in a firm ring, and the cold, blunt claws of some one touched his heart, and sank drowsily into it.

"It pains me!" said the divine Augustus, turning pale. "But look on, Eleazar, look on!"

It seemed as though something, like heavy gates that had been closed from eternity, was slowly opening, and through the widening gap, coldly and quietly, was inflowing the menacing terror of the Infinite. Lo! there entered, as two shadows, infinite emptiness and infinite darkness, and they extinguished the sun, took away the ground from beneath the feet, and the roof from above the head. And the freezing heart ceased to ache.

"Look on, look on, Eleazar!" bade Augustus, staggering.

Time stood still, and the beginning and the end of all things grew horribly near to one another. The throne of Augustus, but lately set up, had already fallen in ruins, and emptiness had taken the place of the throne and of Augustus. Rome noiselessly fell, and a new city appeared in its place, which in its turn was swallowed up by emptiness. Like phantom giants, cities, states and countries fell rapidly and disappeared in emptiness, and, insatiate, the black maw of the Infinite swallowed them up impassably.

"Stop!" bade the Emperor. Already there was indifference in his voice, his hands hung down impotently, and in the vain struggle with approaching darkness his eagle eyes now flamed, now grew dim.

"Thou hast killed me, Eleazar," said he indistinctly and languidly.

But these words of hopelessness saved him.

"No, thou hast not killed me, Eleazar," said he firmly. "But I will kill thee. Be gone!"

That evening the divine Augustus ate and drank with especial hilarity. But at times his hands, as he was lifting them, would stop cold in the air, and a dim glitter would take the place of the bright radiance of his eagle eyes: it was Terror running down in an icy wave through to his very feet. Subdued but not annihilated, coldly awaiting its hour, it stood all his life as a black shadow at his bed-head, in command indeed of the nights, but obediently yielding the bright daylight to the sorrows and joys of life.

Next day, by order of the Emperor, they put out Eleazar's eyes with red-hot irons, and sent him back to his country. The divine Augustus could not make up his mind to put him to death.

So Eleazar returned to the desert, and the desert welcomed him with the whistling breath of the wind, and the burning heat of the sun. Again he sat on a stone lifting upwards his shaggy wild beard, and two black holes in the place of his burned-out eyes looked up to the sky dully and horribly. In the distance the Holy City restlessly hummed and seethed; but near him all was deserted and silent; none approached the place where he who had miraculously risen from the dead was living out his days. His neighbours had long ago abandoned their houses. Driven by the red-hot iron into the depth of his skull, his accursed knowledge lay hidden there as in an ambuscade; and as if from an ambuscade it darted thousands of invisible eyes into a man, so that none dared henceforth to look at Eleazar.

In the evening, when the sun, growing redder and larger, declined towards the west, the blind Eleazar would lingeringly follow it. He would stumble against the stones and, obese and feeble as he was, fall, and then heavily raise himself, and then go on again; and against the red canopy of the twilight his great black body and outstretched arms would bear a monstrous likeness to a cross.

It happened once that he went out, and did not return. And thus ended the second life of Eleazar, who had spent three days in the mysterious power of death, and thence had miraculously risen.

NEW AND STANDARD BOOKS FROM FRANCIS GRIFFITHS' LIST

THE ENGLISH PEOPLE OVERSEAS. A History. By A. WYATT TILBY. To be completed in three volumes. Vol. I. ready. Demy 8vo, cloth. Price 15s. net. In the preface the author says that, "it has been his first principle that no settlement of the English-speaking people overseas should be left unnoticed; and his second that the actors should, as far as possible, speak for themselves from the records they have left behind." He has made a careful study of existing and original authorities: and it is believed that the work will be found both accurate and impartial.

Spectator: "If the later volumes maintain the standard of the first, the completed work should be of the utmost value to those who want the history of the Empire in moderate compass and attractive form."

Globe (Toronto): "The author has such a grasp of his material, and a sense of the picturesque, that he gives a vivid narrative and reflects the atmosphere of the periods described."

THE ROMANCE OF SYMBOLISM. Illustrated. By SIDNEY HEATH. Fcp. 8vo, cloth. Price 7s. 6d. net. The author describes his book as an attempt to arrange in a simple form the principles of Christian symbolism as depicted on the large fabrics, and the minor details, of our churches and cathedrals. Much information is conveyed respecting the symbolical origin and development of ecclesiastical ornament.

WEALTH AND WANT: Studies in Living Contrasts. By W. B. NORTHROP. Crown 8vo, cloth. 5s. net. Illustrated by many unique photographs. The book is a trenchant study of social contrasts by a sincere and powerful writer, who is the coiner of that phrase, "The Deadly Parallel," which is now generally used in connection with glaring social contrasts.

MADEIRA OLD AND NEW. By W. H. KOEBEL. Illustrated with photographs by MISS MILDRED COSSART. Demy 8vo, cloth. 10s. 6d. net. The charm and knowledge which readers have come to expect from the author of "Modern Argentina" are here in evidence. The history and development of Madeira, its manners, customs and scenery are ably presented.

Scotsman: "The author's descriptions of the island, its people and their customs are lively and vivid. The volume is one which may be thoroughly recommended to intending visitors to the island of flowers and fruit. It is, in short, both a useful and entertaining volume."

*

NEW AND STANDARD BOOKS

ENGLISH CHURCH ARCHITECTURE: From the Earliest Times to the Reformation. By G. A. T. MIDDLETON, A.R.I., B.A. Crown 8vo, cloth. 2s. 6d. net.

Dundee Advertiser: "The architect, the ecclesiologist and the antiquary will combine to give Mr. Middleton's handbook a cordial reception. . . . Nothing is wanted to bring home the beauties, proportions and characteristics of our olden time sanctuaries."

THE WESSEX OF ROMANCE. By WILKINSON SHERREN, Author of "The Chronicles of Berthold Darnley," etc. Large 8vo. 6s. net. New and revised edition of a work of value and interest to all lovers of country life and literature. Containing several new illustrations.

Illustrated London News: "It is small wonder that Mr. Wilkinson Sherren's book should have called for a new edition. For his 'Wessex' achieves more than romance—it exhibits humour, imagination and even poetry."

Glasgow Herald: "Mr. Sherren, who has himself recently won a highly honoured place as a story-teller, brings the shrewdness and relish of a fellow-craftsman to his appreciation of Mr. Hardy's novels and poems."

MAN: FIRST AND LAST. From Cave Dweller to Christian. By GEORGE ST. CLAIR, Author of "The Secret of Genesis." Demy 8vo, cloth. 9s. net. The writer of this posthumous book, and of other books having for their purpose the reconcilement of science and the interpretation of ancient myths, died last year before he had time to complete the correction of the proofs of what is undoubtedly a valuable contribution to the study of anthropology. The task has been ably finished by his son.

MODERN ARGENTINA. The El Dorado of To-day. With notes on Uruguay and Chile. By W. H. KOEBEL. With 123 Illustrations. Demy 8vo, cloth, gilt top. Price 12s. 6d. net. The book is concerned not only with the situation—political and commercial—of the Argentine, but with the intimate life of its inhabitants as well. The field afforded by the manners and customs of the modern Argentine has been but little exploited. The study, therefore, of the blending of old and new, of the ethics of the Gaucho knife, and of the temperament of these picturesque riders of the plains, with the up-to-date spirit of enterprise that has come to flood the land, is a fascinating one.

Times: "The book is thoroughly up to date, is very readable, and contains much interesting information. . . . It is the pleasantly written work of a man with observant eye and ready ear who has made the most of his time spent in the country and has succeeded in giving a vivid and intelligent account of what he has seen and heard."

NEW AND STANDARD BOOKS

THE TRUE STORY OF GEORGE ELIOT.
In relation to Adam Bede, giving the life history of the more prominent characters. With 83 Illustrations. By WILLIAM MOTTRAM, grand-nephew of Seth Bede, and cousin to the Author. Large 8vo, gilt top. 7s. 6d. net.

Sphere: "The reading public will welcome anything that throws a light upon its favourite character. We are very grateful to the author for these lucid chapters, and shall read with renewed zest our old favourite 'Adam Bede.' One word as to the excellency of the 'get-up' of the book and the beautiful illustrations which adorn it. They are admirable in every way. The book should command a ready sale, especially among the multitude of lovers of George Eliot's writings."

THE ELEMENTS OF GREEK WORSHIP.
By S. C. KAINES SMITH, M.A. Crown 8vo. Price 2s. 6d. net.

Manchester Guardian: "This admirable little work is referred to by its author as a handbook. The book displays a learning and an intimacy with the most recent research on the subject which render it of the utmost interest and value to the professed student of Greek life and literature."

THE DICKENS CONCORDANCE.
Being a Compendium of Names and Characters and principal places mentioned in all the Works of Charles Dickens. Containing first a List of the Works, secondly a Summary of Chapters in each book or pamphlet, and thirdly a complete Alphabetical Index of Names, with the title of book and number of chapter quoted. By MARY WILLIAMS. Price 3s. 6d. net.

HYDROMEL AND RUE.
Rendered into English from the German of MARIE MADELAINE, by FERDINAND E. KAPPEY. Crown 8vo, cloth, gilt top. Price 5s. net.

SONGS OF OLD FRANCE.
By PERCY ALLEN. Crown 8vo, cloth, gilt top. Price 6s. net.

Scotsman: "Mr. Allen has been noticeably successful in making these verses of philosophical and serious frivolity dance gracefully to the alien music of English. The book should arouse a hearty interest and no little admiration in readers who can understand how Montmartre may relieve the solemn pomposities of the Institute of France."

Daily Telegraph: "The volume will appeal to those who have a taste for romance rendered lyrically; such will feel grateful to Mr. Allen for his selection from French Songs."

A LIFE'S LOVE SONGS AND OTHER POEMS.
By N. THORPE MAYNE. Fcp. 8vo, cloth, gilt top. Price 4s. net.

Scotsman: "Finely chiselled products of metrical art."

NEW AND STANDARD BOOKS

EAST AFRICA AND UGANDA; or, Our Last Land. By J. CATHCART WASON, M.P., with a preface by Sir HARRY JOHNSTON, G.C.M.G., K.C.B. With 33 Illustrations from photographs by Mr. BORUP, of the Church Missionary Society, Uganda; Mr. CUNNINGTON, of Uganda; and Mr. and Mrs. CATHCART WASON. Crown 8vo, cloth, gilt top. Price 3s. 6d. net.

People's Journal: "Mr. Cathcart Wason has published a most entertaining volume on East Africa and Uganda. Sir Harry Johnston has written a most noteworthy preface to the book, which is illustrated by a number of excellent photographs."

IRISH AND ENGLISH PORTRAITS AND IMPRESSIONS. By ROBERT LYND. Crown 8vo, cloth. Price 5s. net.

Daily Chronicle: "Many of the essays have the further charm—so rare in Irish things—the charm of hope."

Pall Mall Gazette: "Mr. Robert Lynd's name must be enrolled among the few English writers who can make their personal impressions vivid and entertaining, as well as sincere and life-like."

THE NEW ORDER: Studies in Unionist Policy. Edited by LORD MALMESBURY. Demy 8vo, cloth. Price 12s. 6d. net. *Contents:* UNIONIST PHILOSOPHY, by Lord Malmesbury. THE CONSTITUTION, 1907, by Lord Morpeth, M.P. IRELAND, by the Hon. Hugh O'Neill. THE HOUSE OF LORDS, by Lord Winterton, M.P. THE PROBLEM OF EMPIRE, by the Hon. Bernhard Wise. HOME INDUSTRIES, by E. G. Spencer Churchill. FOREIGN POLICY, by T. Comyn-Platt. SHIPS, by Alan H. Burgoyne. THE ARMY, by Wilfred Ashley, M.P. THE CITIZEN ARMY, by Henry Page Croft. RELIGIOUS EDUCATION, by Michael H. Temple. LAND, by G. L. Courthope, M.P. SOCIALISM, by Ronald McNeill. LABOUR, by A. D. Steel-Maitland. THE FINANCIAL RESULTS OF FREE TRADE, by Sir J. Rolleston.

Guardian: "The book, as a whole, was well worth publishing, since it shows that among the younger men of the Conservative party, there are independent and original minds which are seriously occupied with the more serious questions of the day and the day after."

ESSAYS ON ART. By JOHN HOPPNER, R.A. Edited by FRANK RUTTER. Fcp. 8vo, cloth. Price 2s. 6d. net. These essays have never been reprinted since their first appearance, a hundred years ago, in reviews of the early 19th century. Hoppner's views on portrait-painting and the art of his contemporaries are expressed with eloquence and sound judgment in these essays, which have been re-discovered and edited with an introduction by Mr. FRANK RUTTER, the art critic of the *Sunday Times*.

NEW AND STANDARD BOOKS

IS A WORLD RELIGION POSSIBLE?
By David Balsillie, M.A. Crown 8vo, 4s. net.

This is a recondite work of great value. Mr. Balsillie has the necessary learning, the logical ability, and the fair-mindedness for his task. In eight chapters he deals with such subjects as the Reconstruction of Belief, Pluralism and Religion, Neo-Hegelian Religion, the Personality of Jesus of Nazareth, the Sayings of Jesus, the True Revelation, and Some Doubtful Sayings of Jesus. He cites Mr. Mallock's and Mr. Campbell's views, and the views of Professor William James and others, and the conclusion he comes to is that a world religion is possible, and that Christianity must be its basis. He states emphatically that he would not derive his materials for a new religion from any doctrines of Science or from any philosophical system, as the latter at any rate better tells what not to believe than what to believe. He would obtain his materials from some concrete realization of the religious ideal, and no better concrete realization in his judgment can be found than that embodied in the personality and teaching of the Founder of Christianity.

Belfast News Letter: "The author has dealt with his subject in a very able and ingenious way, though in doing so he has had to put aside some of the most warmly cherished beliefs regarding religion."

THE SOUL OF ST. PAUL. By the Rev.
A. L. Lilley, Author of "Adventus Regni." 3s. 6d. net.

Daily News: "If all sermons were as good as these there would be no excuse for the falling off in church attendance. They are informed by a deep sense of modern needs, they have a rare fervour even in the printed pages, and throughout one is conscious of a personal charm derived from the preacher's own character and experience. One feels instinctively that what he preaches he has truly lived."

Dundee Advertiser: "The life and what may be called the confessions of St. Paul are brought under review for the purpose of gaining deeper insight into and closer intimacy with the problems which cannot be evaded by any thinking person. As an illustration of Mr. Lilley's teaching, the seeker after comfort—as we all are—is reminded that God's solace is wrung most surely out of the labours and afflictions of the aspiring human soul; that, indeed, hardness and difficulty are the notes of God in human life. This volume will open up to many a new fountain of instruction and strength in the most impressive character in the long history of Christendom."

THE WORLD'S QUEST. Aspects of Christian
Thought in the Modern World. By Rev. F. W. Orde Ward, B.A. Large Crown 8vo, 7s. 6d. net.

Saturday Review: "His pages amply repay study, and will commend themselves to thoughtful people. . . . He has furnished the student, and especially the preacher, with a rich mine of suggestive reading."

NEWMAN, PASCAL, LOISY, and the CATHOLIC CHURCH. By W. J. Williams. Large Crown 8vo, cloth, price 6s. net.

The purpose of the book is to give, in outline, the philosophic basis of the Liberal Catholic movement. It attempts to show that Liberal Catholicism is founded on the best traditions in Catholic thought.

NEW AND STANDARD BOOKS

Cloth 3s. net; by post 3s. 3d.

IS DEATH THE END?

Or, Conscious Personality after Death

BY A WELL-KNOWN AUTHOR

Extract from the Author's Preface

"A question for man, and the most important, is whether his personality involves any element which survives physical death. If a spiritual world exists that has at any time discovered itself to, or offered the means of intercommunication with, humanity, then such a world ought to be discoverable, and capable of entering into relationship with men now.

"The present book is an effort to put into plain language the evidence for conscious personality after death—evidence from Psychical investigation, Philosophy, Science and other thought systems.

"To the question 'Is Death the End?' there are many men who would like an answer not from the pulpit, but from some of the world's front-rank thinkers outside the ranks of theology, because a disinterested witness offers more valued evidence."

In endeavouring to prove his case for a future life, the author devotes a chapter to a summary of the evidence we want, and another to the evidence forthcoming. He goes on to discuss the dawn of the new science and the intercommunication of the two worlds as evidenced by the recent experiments of the Society for Psychical Research and the investigations of individual scientists. In the subsequent chapters he deals with the latent powers of the mind, the state of the dead, recognition after death, and the possibility of new spirit-evidence being produced. Among front-rank witnesses for the case he brings forward the Right Hon. A. J. Balfour, Professor Jevons, Mr. Principal Graham (all of whom he thanks for their help) and others. In the concluding chapter he cites more well-known names in support of the evidence afforded by the senses for the continuity of life after death.

Light:—"The author does not believe in any cessation, at death, of mental or spiritual activity—the soul retains its memories and sympathies: 'those warm sympathies which drew us together are not throttled because the soul possessed of them is nearer the Light and in possession of the great secret'—but he believes in an enlargement of faculty, a wider freedom, a unity of perception, a lightning-like interchange of thought, 'an accurate estimate of our own earth-life's story, an intuitive comprehension, the taking up of a definite work, a progressive happiness in seeking out eternal truths.' Whether giving logically marshalled reasons for his belief, or stating it as an intuitive conviction, the author's attitude is inspiring and encouraging, and we hope that his plainly put reasonings may find a response and be helpful where help is needed."

NEW AND STANDARD BOOKS

A New Work on the Cathedrals of England
OUR ENGLISH CATHEDRALS. By the Rev.
JAMES SIBREE. Fully Illustrated by Photographs and Block Plans. In Two Volumes. Crown 8vo, 5*s*. net each.

"The author has, therefore, thought that there was still room for a book on these wonderful creations of our ancestors' skill and genius, on somewhat different lines from those taken by previous works on the subject." To those who have neither time nor inclination for a minutely detailed examination, the author trusts that this book may be of service; and, "he is not without hope that it may also prove to be of interest to those who, in our own country, or in our Colonies, or in the United States, may wish to have, in a brief and compact form, a sketch of English Cathedrals on the whole."

The book, however, is neither scrappy nor meagre. The buildings are adequately described, building dates and historical notes are given. There is a chapter upon the significance and growth of Gothic Architecture, upon references to the Cathedrals in English Literature (including many quotations), and also upon the relation of our Cathedrals to the life of to-day. The work is complete and thoroughly readable. [*Ready March* 1910.

New Work upon the Legendary Amazons
THE AMAZONS. By G. CADOGAN ROTHERY.
Illustrated. Demy 8vo, 10*s*. 6*d*. net.

Extract from Introductory Chapter.—"Never, perhaps, has the alchemy of Greek genius been more potent than in the matter of the Amazonian myth. It has bestowed a charm on the whole amazing story which has been most prolific in its results; but, unfortunately, by tending to confine it to the narrow vistas of poetry, the intensely interesting psychological aspect has been somewhat obscured. Yet to us the chief value of this myth is due rather to the insight it affords into the mental workings of primitive races, the attitude of man towards that which he dreads but does not fully comprehend, than to the influence of Hellenic art and literature, fruitful in beautiful and humanising manifestation though that influence has been.' [*Ready March* 1910.

A New Illustrated Travel Book
THE UNITED STATES OF BRAZIL. By
CHARLES DOMVILLE-FIFE. Profusely Illustrated. Demy 8vo, 12*s*. 6*d*. net.

The author's extended tour through this vast country, which is still so little known, even through the medium of books, to the majority of English readers, included visits to all the principal towns and States, and a voyage, up the Amazon, into the heart of the country. This book will be found a very interesting and readable consideration of the Brazil of to-day, its history, its cities, its people, and, more especially, its industries, commercial position and outlook. The chapters on these latter subjects alone should make the work well worthy the attention of those who may be considering commercial possibilities or advantages offered them by the rapidly developing American States, and will interest many readers who may not yet have realised the progress attained by this great nation in the making. The opening chapters of the work contain some powerful descriptions, drawn from ancient books, of Old Brazil, its birds and beasts, its legends, the lives of the Jesuit fathers, and the strange, and often diabolical, practices of its early inhabitants, told by actual eye-witnesses of the events, in the quaint and graphic phraseology of the sixteenth and seventeenth centuries. [*Ready February* 1910.

THROUGH TROPIC SEAS. By FRANK BURNETT. Profusely Illustrated. Demy 8vo, 10*s*. 6*d*. net.

A fascinating and graphic account of life and travel in the South Sea Islands of the Pacific. The author, who is thoroughly familiar with his subjects, describes fully the characteristics and history of the Islands, and has much that is interesting to tell concerning the ancient and vanished civilisations of which they were once the home, and concerning the native races; their characters, customs, and legends. The book, which is fully illustrated by photographs, will rank as one of the best upon this subject that have yet appeared. [*Ready March* 1910.

NEW AND STANDARD BOOKS

SUBMARINES OF THE WORLD'S NAVIES.
By CHARLES W. DOMVILLE-FIFE, Designer of the "Fife" Submarine Torpedo Boat (112). Illustrated by 100 Photographs, showing Submarines in Peace and War. Many of these are from exclusive Photographs of Official Trials by the Naval Powers of the World. Crown 4to, 21s. net.
[*Ready February* 1910.

CONTENTS

SUBMARINES IN FUTURE NAVAL WAR. PART I. DESCRIPTION OF EVERY NAVAL SUBMARINE AFLOAT, Classified under the various Naval Powers. *Division into Classes*: Submarines—"Defensive," "Offensive," and Submersibles. *Division into Flotillas*: Depot and Radii of Action of each Vessel. Illustrated by Charts with Reference Tables. Methods employed by the various Naval Powers for Submarine Torpedo-boat attack and defence. Illustrated by Charts. *Types* of Torpedo-boat Destroyers; Torpedo boats and Torpedoes Described and Illustrated. PART II. Submarine Warfare—Construction and Comparison of various Boats. The tactical value of the "Daylight Torpedoboat." Submarine attack and defence tactics. The speed difficulty. "Guns to repel Submarine-boat attack." By Lieut. A. TREVOR DAWSON, R.N. Submarine Construction. Plan—"A Modern Submarine," United States type. Skeleton plans, and key of the principal types. The "Whitehead Torpedo." PART III. The following is a list of some of the Naval Officers, Constructors, and Experts who have contributed to this book of reference. LIFE-SAVING APPLIANCES IN SUBMARINES. With Reference to the Cause of Accidents to Under-Water Craft. Illustrated with exclusive Photographs. SUBMARINES IN FUTURE NAVAL WAR. The progress of the Submarine. By MONS. I. BERTIN, Late Chief Constructor of the French Navy. A NEW FIELD FOR THE TORPEDO. The Value of a Submarine. By Lieut. A. TREVOR DAWSON, R.N. (Messrs. Vickers, Sons & Maxim.) THE ARM OF THE SUBMARINE. The latest "Whitehead" described (40-knots speed). By Captain EDGAR LEES, R.N. (The Whitehead Torpedo Works.) THE DANGERS OF THE SUBMARINE, Real and Imaginary. By LAWRENCE Y. SPEAR, Late Naval Constructor to the United States Navy. SUBMARINE SIGNALLING. With a chapter on the Official Trials. Published by permission of the British Admiralty.

THE NEW MISSION OF ART.
An English rendering by FRANCIS COLMER of the famous Belgian painter, Monsieur Jean Delville's well-known work, with an Introduction. Foreword by CLIFFORD BAX. Illustrated by Reproductions from the Works of Monsieur Delville and other famous Pictures. Demy 8vo, cloth, 7s. 6d. net. [*Ready March* 1910.

A SHORT INTRODUCTION TO THE STUDY OF FRENCH LITERATURE.
By Professor JOHNSON. A critical handbook of the Subject, forming one of the volumes of "The Library of First Principles." Crown 8vo, 2s. 6d. net. [*Ready February* 1910.

MYSTICS AND SAINTS OF ISLAM.
A Series of Biographies, together with a consideration of Sufism and an Introduction. In part Translated from the German by the Rev. CLAUDE FIELD. Crown 8vo, 5s. net. [*Ready March* 1910.

London: FRANCIS GRIFFITHS, 34 Maiden Lane, Strand, W.C.

RETURN TO
LOAN DEPT.

RENEWALS ONLY—TEL. NO. 642-3405
This book is due on the last date stamped below, or
on the date to which renewed.
Renewed books are subject to immediate recall.

OCT 20 1969 1 3

RECEIVED
JAN 27 '70 -11 AM
LOAN DEPT.

RECEIVED
OCT 8 '69
LOAN DEPT.

FEB 10 1970 46

23 1970 12

JUN 5 '74 35

REC'D CIRC DEPT
23 1970 17

Due end of FALL Quarter
Subject to recall after —

DEC 8 '70

RECEIVED
FEB 10 '70 -4 PM
LOAN DEPT.

REC'D LD   DEC 9 '70 -3 PM 4

LD21A-60m-6,'69
(J9096s10)476–A-32

General Library
University of California
Berkeley

Printed in Great Britain
by Amazon